A Landlord's Tale

A Landlord's Tale

Gammy L. Singer

Dafina Books

KENSINGTON PUBLISHING CORP.
http://www.kensingtonbooks.com

This book is a work of fiction. Names, characters, businesses, organizations, places, events and incidents either are a product of the author's imagination or are used fictitiously. Any resemblance to actual persons, living or dead, is purely coincidental.

DAFINA BOOKS are published by

Kensington Publishing Corp.
850 Third Avenue
New York, NY 10022

All Kensington titles, imprints and distributed lines are available at special quantity discounts for bulk purchases for sales promotion, premiums, fund-raising, educational or institutional use.

Special book excerpts or customized printings can also be created to fit specific needs. For details, write or phone the office of the Kensington Special Sales Manager: Kensington Publishing Corp., 850 Third Avenue, New York, NY 10022. Attn. Special Sales Department. Phone: 1-800-221-2647.

Dafina and the Dafina logo Reg. U.S. Pat. & TM Off.

ISBN 0-7582-0893-6

First Kensington Trade Paperback Printing: March 2005
10 9 8 7 6 5 4 3 2

Printed in the United States of America

ACKNOWLEDGMENTS

Overwhelming gratitude to friend and mentor Patrick Picciarelli, who has always been in my corner; mentor Ed Dee; agent Frank Weimann; and editor Karen Thomas and the Kensington family.

Thanks to my own landlord, David Howson, who provided insight, knowledge, and anecdotal tales about Harlem village during the 70s, and to Norman Blake, who provided more of the same. Also many thanks to lawyer Bob Fletcher, who gave me information about New York City's real estate laws, and buddy Henry G. Sanders for his poker expertise.

Moreover, I am grateful for scholarship assistance from the Screen Actors Guild Foundation and the Actors Fund, and I also remain especially appreciative of the help and instruction from the teachers, staff, and former students in Seton Hill University's Writing Popular Fiction master's degree program. This novel is the result of that program.

Finally, I wouldn't be where I am today were it not for the support and love of The Women, my buddies, who have been by my side, for lo these many years—Margaret Avery, Michelle Davison, Wendy Fairbanks, Ernestine Jackson, and Emily Yancy, and of course, my daughter, Laetitia Russ. They have always encouraged every dipsy-doodle project I've devised and every mountain I've wanted to climb. I dedicate this book to all of them.

Chapter 1

My eyes weren't fixed on the direction I was driving, but on the words NIGGER LANDLORD slashed in bright neon paint across the ribs of the oak tree that stood in front of my new home. And on the woman who waited with arms crossed and meaty butt spread against the iron railing that led up the stoop to the front door.

I yanked back the steering wheel of my nine-month-old Baby, a '76 cranberry Cadillac Seville, as it jumped the curb, scraped rubber, and screeched to a halt in front of 247 W. 128th Street.

Shit. The gun tucked inside the waistband of my pants slid to my crotch as the car rocked to a stop. A toaster and a tangle of shirts, jackets, and ties tumbled onto the front seat. I threw clothes off me with one hand and dug around in my pants like a pervert with the other while the woman on the stoop with the ham-hocks butt gave me the evil eye. Jesus, lucky I didn't shoot my damn nuts off.

I had given up my lease at my Sugar Hill crib. Lack of money was the reason. And I'd just come from Bunky's Pawnshop where I had divested myself of most of my earthly possessions. The rest I'd piled high in the back seat—now they were in the front.

I hoped Hocks couldn't see what I was doing. I retrieved the gun and tucked it under the seat and slammed out of the car. Trouble comes in threes, like death. At this moment Harry the Monkey Chaser was number two, which was the reason I was carrying. I glanced at the woman. Was she number three?

I marched around to Baby's polished chrome bumper and bent down to inspect the whitewalls. Out of the corner of my eye I saw the woman slide her butt off the railing and roll like a tank toward me.

"You the landlord?" she asked.

Her question was as weighty as she was. I reserved my answer. Street life had taught me to be wary. If I'da been a dog, my ears would have flattened back against my head and I would have growled at her approach, but I was an entrepreneur now, owner of two brownstones willed to me by my father, so I was cool. Don't let her be somebody else I owed.

"I axed you if you was the landlord."

She was all up on me now. I could see she was frayed around the edges. I stepped back to let air come between us. The sour smell of her breath almost knocked me over.

"You *that* landlord?" she said, pointing to the tree.

"Why you asking?"

"I'm looking to rent a room is why. Is you the landlord or not?"

I shrugged the woman off, opened my car, slipped the gun into the pocket of my coat, and said, "I don't rent to no big-butt women." And hoped that would end the conversation.

"Well, fuck you, too. Looka here, mister, I ain't the one wrote on your motherfucking tree, so don't be fucking taking that shit out on me."

She had a point, but I didn't let her know that. I set the burglar alarm, locked the car door, and proceeded up the steps to my brownstone. Her last "hey" came at me like a bear breaking wind.

"Hey," she repeated, "you got a dollar on you? Since you ain't renting, Mr. Nigger Landlord, whyn't you give me some change so's I can ride crosstown to check me out a room over there?"

I turned. The woman was crazy.

"The name is Amos Brown," I said and shook my head in amazement at her audacity. And then, I don't know why, but I busted out laughing—at her, at me, at the tree, at the whole fucking mess I had got myself into. If it had been her that owed Harry the Monkey Chaser six thousand dollars, would she care? Hell no. It'd be Harry's problem, not hers.

There she stood, hands on hips, expecting me and the universe to cough up her daily bread. And we would.

I said, "Hell, woman, you ain't even got money for transportation to get across town. How you think you going to pay for any room?"

It was her turn to laugh and I saw the parking space where her front teeth had been.

"Social Services, they help me out. Now, honey, believe me when I tell you I can *get* the rent. I *knows* how to do that."

"I'll bet you sure enough do." I dug into my pocket, extracted a silver dollar, and flipped it to her. She flapped her hands together like a trained seal, and caught the coin between her lips. Amazing. Tucking it into her bra, she grinned her appreciation at me.

"What you say, Nigger Landlord. You all right," she said. "Yes, sir, you all right."

"Amos."

But she didn't hear me. She was stepping fast. Probably beating a path to Sam's Liquor Store located around the corner on Lenox Avenue.

I stood there for a while, hands tucked in my pant pockets. Life hummed along the length of the busy block. It was late spring, and sprouting cherry blossoms graced the branches of the trees on both sides of the street. Children played catch, and rode their bicycles and scooters in and out of the spaces made by cars parked along the street. Looked like Anytown, U.S.A., except it wasn't. It was a suffering Harlem. Beyond the trees ornamented with blossoms were signs of a decaying community. Abandoned buildings and boarded-up houses with locked-away memories of Harlem were scattered among the occupied residences. I breathed the street. This street was me.

My Harlem. Born and bred here and proud of it. The facades of the buildings were weathered, but there was a grandeur that lingered, waiting to be revived, spruced up, ready to go again. Like me, I guess.

I glanced up at the tree. A child's drawstring purse, colored red, dripped like blood off one of its branches. I reached up and pulled it down and inspected the contents—a collection of feathers and small stones. I smiled. Play money, I'd bet, and didn't I wish I had some. Money to play with. I slipped the tiny bag into my pocket. Probably belonged to one of my tenants' kids.

Hard luck had been on my butt like a dog in heat, and I didn't have anybody to blame but myself. That's the natural truth. Trouble Number One, like a gathering hurricane, knocked me off my feet and wiped my ass out. My numbers operation crashed and burned, my bride of six months disappeared soon as the money went, and my gambling spun horribly out of control.

Now Harry the Monkey Chaser and his boys were looking for me. Number Two, no shit, the man wanted his money. Simple. And I didn't have it. That was simple too. So like Job, I wondered when the next axe would fall—Trouble Number Three. All I needed was a little time; I'd get it together. I had never chiseled on a bet before, and I wasn't starting now. But Harry was impatient. He didn't want to wait for leaves to blossom.

In my mind, a guitar twanged, and a bluesman sang, "Blues, stay away from my door." I touched the weapon in my pocket, looked to the right and left, then entered the three-story brownstone. News travels fast in Harlem. How soon before Harry caught up with me? How soon before the next axe fell?

Chapter 2

The parlor room of the brownstone was the office because it faced the street, and every gambler knew that was the best place to be. I stood inside the room with its detailed antique molding and high ceilings, and looked through a tall window onto the street below. The window and its twin extended from floorboard to ceiling and faced the front. Lodged between the two was an ornate gilt-edged mirror, running the full length of the windows.

I watched, as I suppose my father did before me, the people passing by. I could also see the comings and goings in my brownstone across the way. My father left me that one too. Although 128th Street wasn't an artery, for nearly all hours of the day foot traffic was as steady as a heartbeat and always interesting to watch.

School children and hookers, lovers old and young, the employed and the unemployed—all did their stroll down 128th Street. The destitute and the homeless? Yeah, them too, you could see them any time of the day, wandering or weaving up one side of the street and down the other. Nobody bothered them much.

One thing I couldn't take, though, was the drug dealers and their strung-out clients. Anybody else and their mama I could pretty well accommodate in my world, but those fiends . . . man, they slinked in shadows like ghouls and gave me the fucking heebie-jeebies.

I'll tell you this—their ass was grass if I caught any of them hanging around. Drugs were eating up Harlem and it wasn't pretty. Hell, drugs were as much the reason for boarded-up buildings as anything else going on in Harlem, no matter what those mucketymuck black politicians wanted the world to hear.

People I used to deal with every day in my numbers business just weren't civilized anymore, because of drugs. That's why I quit. The criminals and even the cops didn't act like they used to back in the day. Both sides had gone crazy. Street rules were murky. All of Harlem had turned ugly with drugs. I was thirty-eight and through with it.

Thanks to my dear departed father—so what if the fucker was a bastard—I had the opportunity to turn legit and I took it.

I eased my large frame into the swivel chair in front of my desk and heaved a sigh. Now if I could just get this gambling jones off my back.

I heard a knock on the door, and without so much as a lookyhere, a grizzled dwarf burst into the room and announced, "I ain't trying to get into your business, but I wouldn't leave them things you got in your car too long out there on the street. Harlem-town ain't what it used to be, you know."

"Who the hell are you and how did you get in here?"

"I'm the super of your buildings and I used my key, that's how. Name's Seltzer. I come by for my pay, and to tell you that some varmint done made off with my dog Susie and I expect to be compensated. Though, dang it, there ain't enough money in the world that can replace my Susie."

"What the hell you talking about? Wait a minute, wait just a minute, how come this is the first time I laid eyes on you?"

"I expect it's 'cause you a night bird, and I rises with the chickens."

"I ain't never seen you do nothing around here."

"That's 'cause you ain't been looking. You damn sure can't see what you ain't been looking for. Who you think been sweeping up, clearing up, and cleaning up around here?"

That got me.

"To tell you the truth, I hadn't thought about it."

"Yeah, well, time to think, and time to pay up."

I guess he was right about that, but cash flow was a problem now, and I told him so.

"What, your daddy didn't leave you no money 'long with these houses?"

I shook my head.

"Well, shit, best you start collectin' some rent, 'cause my wife, my children, my dog, and me all need money to live on. I ain't worked for your father for free, and I damn sure ain't working for no pup like you for free."

"Well, Mr. Seltzer—"

"Selzter ain't no last name. Name's James. James Pope, I just go by Seltzer."

"Okay, Seltzer then, I wish I could fix you up, brother. I really do. I've been a landlord for two months and five days, but so far only two people have been by to pay any rent. The fag upstairs and Miss Ellie across the street."

"Son, is you crazy? They ain't going to come to you—you got to go to them. Rise up early in the morning and knock on their door. Some of these folk be working, you know. If you don't know nothing, you better ask somebody. You don't look stupid, boy, but you sure is acting stupid."

With that remark, he crossed the line. My eyes tightened. I wasn't used to no dwarf insulting me.

"Just so you don't forget, I'm the one paying you a salary, remember?"

"Uh-uh, not yet, you ain't. And looka here, you a big tree, but big trees can be cut down, hear me?"

He frothed a little at the mouth as he spat out the words. I suddenly understood why he was called Seltzer. And then, can you believe it? This little cat whipped out a switchblade on me. I knew it had to be for effect. He couldn't be for real. He hiked up his pants and revved his engine.

"I don't play, see? I'm a country boy from West Virginia, but I can slice me up a nigger as quick as I can gut a pig."

He was spinning and churning like a wind-up toy. The whiskers on his face bristled, and his big nose started twitching. For the second time that day, I laughed my ass off. The little shit looked so funny I laughed until tears rolled down my cheeks.

He said, "I ain't playing with you."

That's when I gagged on my saliva. "Yeah, yeah, I hear you, old man." I kicked my right leg up in the air, and knocked the knife out of his hand, and grabbed for it before he could. "And I can ram this knife up your ass quicker than you can say ouch, don't hurt me. Now what you got to say about that?"

He looked at me.

"I guess I ain't got nothing to say. You big, but you quick."

I wiped tears from my eyes and was still chuckling when I closed the knife and tossed it back to him.

"Don't wolf at the wolf," I said. "Don't mess with the big dog, because I'm ready for your ass."

Then I patted his shoulder and said, "And if you don't know, you better ask somebody."

I roared again. I was six three, dusting the underside of two hundred pounds, and this termite's head hardly reached my chest. But I liked the old man's style and the game we were playing. He was letting me know I should respect him. I was okay with that.

"I can tell, Selz, we're going to get along just fine."

Then he twisted up his face as if it hurt and said, "Never mind that, big *dog*—just collect some rent, youngster, and get me my money 'fore I be forced to hurt you."

"How much you worth, old man?"

"How much you got?"

"If you worth what I got, you ain't worth much."

"Well, I expect two hundred a month for my services, and you owe me for two months."

"And what would those services be?"

"I fix what's broke, put the trash out on collection days, and generally clean up around here."

"Then the next rent I collect is yours. If I can figure out who owes what for how long and who's actually living here. Montcrieff was bad at record keeping."

I picked up a ledger from the desk.

"I found this under a pile of junk, but it doesn't do me any good because he's put different rent amounts for the same person and the man stopped making entries in here three years ago. And lease agreements? Forget about it."

"I tell you what. You make up a figure, high as you want, and ask your tenants for it, and I'll bet a dollar to a doughnut, every last one of them will dig up their lease agreement to prove you wrong."

"Good idea, old man."

And then we laughed and chimed together, "If you don't know, you better ask somebody."

"Speaking of that—you have an idea who loves me so much they want to write love letters across a tree?"

Next I indicated the room.

"And got any ideas what I can do with this mess?"

"No to the first question—probably some drunk with nothing to do. I'll try to get something to take it off. This here junk gonna have to wait. I got too much else to do. Anyway, you got the rest of your life. What you doing with it? Why don't you clean out a room?"

He smirked and I rolled my eyes at him. I had organized the desk and bought a new filing cabinet. But the rest of the room looked as if an explosion had taken place. A dusty filing cabinet stood against one wall, stuffed with everything except the paper you'd expect to be in there—string, wire, canned foods, rat poison, everything. Buckets of paint, tools, rusted pipes, an old commode, lightbulbs, doors, fuses, condoms, and a bit of everything else was jammed into the rest of the space, in every nook and cranny and spread across every surface.

"It'll take the rest of my life," I replied.

Seltzer started to leave, then turned at the door and said, "Tell you what, though, I am going to cut me the somebody who walked off with my sweet Susie. I know that dog. She wouldn't have gone easy."

He paused.

"Maybe they killed her."

He turned his head away from me and drew his sleeve across his nose.

I thought, *oh, shit, if he's crying, I'm leaving.*

"Had her guarding the basement across the street for the last two days," he said, then looked back up at me. "You know a squatter's been living there?"

I nodded, overjoyed that he'd pulled himself together.

And then he held out his hand, palm up. "Pipe's busted across the street. Water's leaking. Need to replace the pipe and replaster the wall."

I reached into my back pocket. Yes, I knew about the squatters.

Empty take-out boxes of Chinese food and trash lay strewn on the floor alongside filthy mattresses that still carried the stench of wretched humanity. I put locks on both doors, only to see the rooms trashed again the following week, and the locks broken.

"Yeah, locks didn't do no good," I said.

I also knew about Susie. It was me that called the ASPCA to come get the vicious mutt. A fucking Great Dane. Can you believe it? Her paws were as big as my feet. The animal had lunged at me when I entered the basement apartment. I thought the squatters had left the dog there. Since I'm not a fool I didn't mention this fact to Seltzer.

I looked down at his outstretched hand, sighed, peeled some bills off the roll from my pocket, and gave them to him. I had hocked ten of my three-piece suits at Bunky's for a lousy three hundred bucks—custom-made, too—and that accounted for what money I possessed at the moment, and was all that stood between me and the poorhouse. I had meant to chill Harry down with the money as a good-faith payment until I could lay my hands on some more bread.

"Thanks," he said and eyed the remaining money in my hand. I stuffed the bills back into my pocket.

He moved to the door. "I'll pick up the supplies today and bring you your change—if there is any. I'll start on the work tomorrow. Ain't playing about that stuff in your car. You better get it out 'fore it's gone. You moving in?"

I nodded. "Don't have a choice."

"Well, number four was your dad's. Stuff's all gone. Plenty of room. I'll paint it up for you."

"Better paint those basement apartments across the street first. They look like shit. Want to hurry up and rent them out."

He held out his hand again, and reluctantly I threw some more bills into it.

"Seltzer, man, I'll tighten you up soon as I collect some rent, okay?"

He nodded and left the room. The door slammed behind him.

I gnawed my lip and made a decision. The unpacking would have to wait. I threw on my jacket and headed out. Guess I have to go see a man about a dog.

Chapter 3

Saturday morning and I was up early, all shit-shaved-and-bathed, and crossed the street to see whether Seltzer had started working on the apartments yet. I saw a pile of refuse stacked up outside the building, so I figured he was there. I descended into the basement when I heard the low growl of the demon dog Susie, who crouched and slinked her butt toward me.

"Seltzer," I called. "Come get your damn dog. I'm coming in."

Big old dumb-ass dog, she forgot already who had saved her ass. Yesterday, she had licked and lapped all over me in the car. Just like a bitch. Fickle.

Seltzer appeared around the corner.

"Susie, come here, girl. You don't want to poison yourself with no tough meat. Don't bite the man, come over here, girl."

"I wish that dog would bite me. I'd shred her ass through a meat grinder."

Susie growled again. She didn't like what I said.

"Hey, old dog, I'm just fooling with you, come here, you rotten spoiled thing."

I held out my hands, and her dog brain remembered who had previously fondled her. She let me rub her hard behind her ears. Her tail was whipping her to death, and she slurped her tongue in pure joy.

"Funny how old Susie just come back by herself," Seltzer said.

"How's that funny? She probably let herself out to take a leak and get a little nookie and got locked out."

"Yeah," said Seltzer, "you probably right. That's one smart dog though, you got to admit. Not only did she let herself back in, she locked the doors behind her, changed her water, and fed herself. Yessir, you can't get no smarter than that."

"Sure can't. That's one smart dog. Listen, she's back, ain't she? You ought to be grateful."

"Oh, I am, I am. And I don't have to cut me no nigger."

I rolled my eyes at him and stepped inside the front apartment.

"Paint job looks good."

"Yeah, almost finished with this one. Get to the other one tomorrow. If you hurry up and rent this place, won't have to worry about squatters. I'll get to your apartment on Monday."

"No problem, man."

I went to the rear studio apartment and opened the door. Susie bolted past me and began sniffing the wall. I looked around. The rooms had been cleared out, but a damp smell hung in the air. Susie kept sniffing at the wall.

"Seltzer, Susie ain't about to piss on the wall, is she? That's all we need in here."

We both looked at Susie. Now she was pawing at the wall. Then she growled and crunched plaster between her teeth.

Seltzer moved to her. "Susie, what the hell you doing? Come here, girl." He took her by the collar and pulled her away from the wall.

"What you got, girl, huh? What you got?"

He leaned closer to the wall to inspect.

"Jesus, Amos, come here."

"What's the matter?" I said and stepped to the wall.

"What's that look like to you?"

I looked and then I touched the wall. It was damp. The second-floor leak must have traveled down to the basement and loosened the plaster. Parts of it had chipped away, leaving a sizeable hole, *and* a bone sticking out of the wall. I touched it gingerly.

"What'll we do now, boss?"

I looked at Seltzer, then back at the bone. "Fuck I know. Call the police?"

I edged closer and knelt down. "Looks like bone from someone's leg. And this . . ." I rubbed a fragment of cloth lodged in the wall. ". . . This looks like a piece of a dress."

Chapter 4

First squad car that showed up from the Twenty-eighth Precinct, I knew one of the cops. He was a brother that used to live over on East 130th Street. I knew his mama and his daddy. Both of them played the numbers every day. Curtis Charles, his name was. He looked good in his uniform. Good to see a brother making something of himself. He was surprised that I was the landlord. I was starting to get used to that. Whole lot of people were surprised, myself included.

Curtis and his partner fooled around inside the apartment, asked us a few questions, then strung yellow tape across the entrance to the basement, keeping me and everybody else out. That was okay with me. I wasn't one of the morbidly curious.

Susie, Selz, and me waited out on the front stoop of the brownstone. The news spread fast. The neighbors collected on the sidewalk as if they were waiting for the Second Coming or the Macy's Thanksgiving Day Parade. Honest to God, one woman brought a beach chair and lunch, introduced herself as Mabel, and sat on the sidewalk and talked to everyone and their mama about what was going on. It was like a block party and everyone showed up.

Fortunate for me, most of the tenants were nosy, too. Seltzer introduced me to a bunch of them, and I started collecting rents right there on the stoop. Wasn't rolling in dough, though. As fast as I raked it in with one hand, Seltzer took it from the other.

Counting both buildings, I had seven apartments empty. Each of the brownstones had been cut up into eight apartments, and with rent control that meant profits were pitiful.

My oldest tenant was Miss Ellie, a former Cotton Club dancer. Next in age, Seltzer said, was Zeke, an old guy with a sour disposition who used to be best friends with my father. Huh, as far as I was concerned, that information was all that was needed to explain Zeke's personality defect. The man got real hostile when I asked him for the rent. He stomped his cane down next to my foot, almost nipped my toe, then took off in a fury down the street.

I didn't know what the old guy's problem was, but we sure as hell were going to have to talk.

Winnie Martin, who had dimples in her cheeks and probably in her butt as well, brought me some food with her rent money. She passed potato salad and barbecue ribs among all of us who had settled on the stoop.

The Fag (Wilbur was his real name, and it looked like I was going to have to start using it) knew a social occasion when he saw it and flew out of the brownstone front door in a flowing robe, and flitted among the crowd like A'Lelia Walker or one of them other famous hostesses and served people potato chips. I had to admit he wasn't a bad sort, and in fact, he was kind of funny. The other kind of funny, you know, comical.

Wilbur was tall and thin with keen features and long processed hair that he was currently flipping all over the chip bowl. Came up here from Texas—where men were men, he told me—and that's why he had to leave. He asked straight out if his sexual persuasion—his words—was going to be a problem. I told him hell no. His money would spend just like everybody else's. He thanked me and left me a cake.

I felt a tap on my shoulder. Miss Ellie had appeared like the star she was and eased her petite frame down beside me on the stoop. I couldn't believe my eyes. I had more wrinkles than she did. She wore carefully applied makeup and had herself perched atop the highest heels I had ever seen, and I knew the woman was old enough to be my grandmother.

"You got the rent for this month, Miss Ellie?"

"Listen, boy, and you'd better write this down—my Social Security comes the fifteenth of every month. You catch me then, or you don't catch me at all."

She leaned away from me and looked me up and down. I found myself blushing. Jesus.

She noticed my discomfort, but decided to overlook it.

"Boy, don't mind me. I'm just noticing how much you resemble your father. He was handsome, you know. Tall Negro, had high cheekbones and a big old square jaw just like yours."

When she said "jaw" she reached for mine and squeezed it tight between her fingers and waggled my head back and forth. I let her have her jollies for a few seconds, then I unclamped her fingers from around my jaw.

Seltzer informed me his day ended at two and he was taking Susie and going on home. The cops didn't stop him, so it must have been okay, although, hell, if I was them I would've held Susie as a material witness.

By the time the second police car drove up, and the police pulled me to the side and questioned me again, I got the idea that my apartment might be tied up for more than a day. The cops were frustrated that I wasn't giving them more answers, but I was doing the best I could.

"Look," I repeated to Detective Bundt, "I have no information on who lived here before or how long. I don't even know how long that basement apartment's been unoccupied. I'm new at this, give me a break."

He slid his eyes over me, wrote something down, and moved on to the next subject.

"How long has your father been dead?"

"Maybe five months now."

The other detective butted in, "He have a good relationship with his tenants?"

"I don't know."

"Why not?"

"Because I didn't have a good relationship with him. I never knew my father. I saw him once when I was twelve."

Bundt raised his eyebrows, but that was all. Two other police vehicles had pulled up, one was a van. He said to the other cop, "Okay, Caporelli, let's wrap this up here."

And then to me, "Mr. Brown, the police are probably going to be working here for a couple of days. We're sure it's human remains. The skeleton is lodged in cement and that's a problem. Got some people coming now who are going to help us figure out what to do about that. We'll let you know what we decide, sir. We'll try not to be a bother, but you do understand, we got our jobs to do."

Did I understand? Was a pig's pussy pork? If he only knew. I was elated at the news. And I liked the way they called me "sir." Must have something to do with me being a homeowner. And police protection, too? Harry won't try to fuck with me with the cops around. I could've kissed Bundt smack on his lips, Caporelli, too.

"I understand. You'll have my full cooperation."

And I meant that.

Oh yeah, and the squatters would be losing their nest. Things were looking up.

Chapter 5

Six days later the tape was still there. All the tenants in the brownstone across the street had been complaining. The police had used jackhammers, drills, and God knows what else on the wall of the basement, and as far as I knew, they still hadn't removed the skeleton. If they wanted to bring it in one piece to their lab, they had to take out a concrete chunk of wall to do it. The whole situation seemed kind of absurd to me, but I had other things to think about and the skeleton was the least of my worries.

Now that the tenants knew me, and knew where to find me, they were real comfortable about seeking me out any time of the day or night. Since most of them had paid their rent, their demands accelerated and they felt I owed them.

Zeke, with his no-rent-paying ass, had the balls to complain about a leaking toilet, but would he let Seltzer in to fix it? Of course not. I suspected his place was a rat's nest that he didn't want disturbed.

Seltz told me that he personally hadn't crossed the man's threshold in over twenty-plus years. Zeke allowed only a select few to enter his domain. So Selz slipped him tools through a cracked door and the nut fixed the toilet himself. Good. Anyway, Seltzer was kept hopping and so was I. I finally had to announce office hours and tacked a sign on my door to that effect.

Today I was working on cleaning out the office. Seltzer worked upstairs, painting the hallway. Most of the big stuff had been cleared out of the office. Thank God that rusty commode had been removed.

I sorted out the bales of junk inside the old bureau dresser that stood in the corner. Had two piles in front of me. *Keep* and *Go*. The Go pile looked like the Eiffel Tower. The smell of paint hung heavy in the air and reminded me that money was going out faster than it was coming in. Both buildings needed a lot of work and the clock was ticking. I wasn't close to six hundred, let alone six thousand, dollars.

The brownstone was getting unwanted publicity, too. Ever since the story about the skeleton came out in the *New York Times*, all kinds of city inspectors discovered me and descended on this building like rabid wolves.

The fire inspector bugged me the most. The work he wanted me to do was going to cost me a couple of grand. As soon as I heard "refit the sprinkler heads, install fire alarms," I stopped paying attention. But I didn't miss his wink, or his not so subtle request for me to grease his palm. No way was I going to play *Let's Make a Deal* with this turkey. I had principles after all—and by the way, a lack of money.

He wrote up a couple of violations, handed them to me, and told me to make an appointment with the Department of Housing Preservation and Development, HPD. Right away I knew the deal was not going to be about me preserving anything *I* owned.

I was mucking around in the bureau when I ran across a red velvet bag stashed in the bottom drawer. I pulled it out and, curious, rummaged through its contents. Jesus. My hand closed around a twelve-inch-long pink rubber dick that was decorated with veins and everything. There was even pubic hair attached in weepy tufts on the base of it.

A light tap-tap-tap sounded at the door of my office, and a mouse of a voice called my name.

I jumped, startled, threw the dick on the Go pile, and shouted, "Come in."

Patty, second floor rear, edged through the door with her two-year-old, Josephine, on her hip. She inched her body into the room, like she was afraid of taking up too much space. The baby had crammed half her little fist into her mouth, and her head rested quiet against her mother's shoulder.

The pink dick seemed to glow from the Go pile. My face got hot. I hoped Patty didn't notice.

"Mr. Brown?"

"Yeah, what can I do for you?"

Patty was thin as a piece of spaghetti, not more than nineteen years old, with Jell-O pudding chocolate skin and defeated eyes. I waited. Everything about her said *I can't pay you this month.*

"Uh, Mr. Brown," she said, "I can't pay you this month. My check ain't come, and I ain't been able to get down to Social Services offices 'cause of Josephine being sick. And I can't never get nobody on the phone as hard as I be trying. They won't answer they phone."

Since I had called about five city offices myself this week, including the HPD, I could relate.

"It's okay. I can wait." Where in the hell did that come from? That was the biggest lie I'd told all day. "How's the little one doing?"

"Um . . . not so good. I don't know what's wrong with her. She ain't eating, don't even cry much."

"You taken her to the doctor?"

"Uh . . . not yet."

"What you waiting on?" I guess I barked at her. She jumped back nearly a foot and pressed herself into the woodwork. Mute, she stared at me with round eyes. I sighed. She was as much child as the baby she carried.

I lowered the volume on my voice box. "Get a jacket, and something to put over the baby. I'll take you around to Harlem Hospital. Josephine needs to be looked at."

She scurried out the door. I put on my jacket, stuffed the pink dick into a trash bag, and looked for my keys.

Five minutes later I was still looking. Patty waited patiently in the hall. Okay, okay, so everybody has failings. Gambling and losing keys happened to be two of the many I had. I stood stock-still as a realization hit me. I hadn't shot craps, played a horse, or even thought about getting into a poker game for weeks now.

Hmm . . . and it wasn't about money or the lack of it. That never stopped me before. I'd been too damn busy, that was it. A smile swished around my insides. Tickled the hell out of me, and then I remembered—the new key chain. It had caught my eye at Bunky's and I'd traded a pair of cuff links for it. I was embarrassed thinking about it now. Me, the guy who used to throw thousands of dollars around—there I was, at Bunky's Pawnshop, haggling with Bunky for a damn talking key chain.

I charged around the office and clapped like crazy. I held my hands high in the air and clapped. I hunched over and clapped around my toes. Damn, all I needed was taps on my shoes and a sombrero on my head and I could have been one of those fucking flamenco types.

Patty peeked through the door. Her eyes went round again. I was a wild man. I clapped in the corners and all over the fucking room until I heard it—finally.

Irritating as hell. "I'm right here. I'm right here," it said between each clap. I moved toward the sound. It came from inside the coffee mug on the top of my desk.

Success. I pounced on the cup and retrieved my keys. I also plucked up the small red purse that sat next to the cup—might as well give it to little Josie, no one else had claimed it—and then I exited the office.

Before Patty could muster a question, I whisked her and the baby out to my car, and ignored the puzzled expression on Patty's face.

Chapter 6

I didn't get back to the brownstone until eight that evening and jumped into the shower. It took a lot of scrubbing to wash away the day. The doctors at the hospital had kept Patty's baby. Something serious was going on. They wanted to run tests. When they told her, Patty's thin form broke in two like a pencil snapping. I felt bad for her so I told her I'd help her out and take her down to Social Services on Monday.

During that short trip to and from the hospital I became aware that I needed a change of scenery in the worst way. I had been cooped up for a week. *Hiding*. I made myself say the word as I shaved, and I looked at myself in the bathroom mirror while I said it. What was I, a punk? I had to face up to Harry sooner or later. Monday. I'd seek him out on Monday.

Restless and butt-naked, I wandered around the apartment, glanced at my few sticks of furniture, trolled the books scattered everywhere—hey, I was a reader, what can I tell you?—and finally made up my mind to get out. After all, it was Saturday night.

I hauled clothes out of the closet and started to dress. Now, it wasn't on my great mind, but damn, must have been on my little mind, because I had trouble pushing that stiff mind over to my right pant leg as I pulled on my brown slacks. Another revelation—hadn't had an oil change or a lube job in a great while, and I sure wasn't talking about no cars. Maybe I'd get lucky tonight.

My scaled-down wardrobe was a definite handicap, but I jumped sharp as I could. Piss on that fucking Bunky anyhow. I imagined I saw Bunky, his thin face, like a cadaver, staring back at me from the closet door mirror. The sucker had on one of my three-piece suits. I shuddered and shook off the vision.

I pulled a splashy brown and turquoise tie from the closet and wrapped it around the collar of my beige shirt, and slipped into a conservative mud-brown jacket.

Believe me, in my dog days, looking my worst, I wouldn't be caught dead looking like some pimp, not me. *Esquire/GQ* was more my style and my taste. Had to have something going for me. Never thought my looks could corral a chicken, and knew I wasn't too swift in the conversation department. But for some reason I had had my share of women. Go figure.

Too bad they moved in and out of my life like a revolving door. I straightened my tie. The voice of my soon-to-be-ex whined in my ear, "You never want to *communicate* with me." I shuddered at the memory. Damn straight. Once I wanted to. I did. But I found I couldn't.

Shit, I must be getting cabin fever. What was the matter with me? I pushed both Bunky and the whiner down a coal chute and off my mind. Let me out of here.

I peered into the mirror. I looked okay. Maybe even good. That had to be enough. I splashed cologne on my neck and slapped my cheeks. That snapped me back to reality.

A tuneless tune whistled through my lips and I snatched my money clip off the dresser and grinned as I headed for the door. I halted midway, patted all my pockets—then I roamed the apartment for another ten minutes, clapping and looking for my damn keys.

Chapter 7

I slid a Muddy Waters tape into Baby's tape deck and headed down to 125th Street, then cruised west. Muddy's guitar twanged, and his blues got all into my underwear. But after a minute I opted for something more upbeat, so I replaced Muddy with Sam Cooke.

Sam sang "Someday a Change Is Gonna Come," the song that was practically the civil rights anthem, and I got the message. "You fucking-A," I said, and thumped a responsive amen on the steering wheel.

It was a five-minute drive to Showman's. I pulled up opposite the club, parked, and started across the street. The place was still holding on, a part of old Harlem, and still a popular place. It had been around since the late forties. Wells and the Lenox Lounge were open too, but they were faded memories of what they used to be. And now the happening jazz of the sixties had moved like a tidal wave downtown, pulling its devoted disciples with it—both black and white.

A shame, I thought, but like Sam says, a change gonna come, and like a wheel, the music will roll back just like everything else. Got to believe that. Music to Harlem is like butter to bread. And Harlem ain't dead. Not yet, anyways.

From way outside the door I heard the music. The Hammond organ wailed and screamed into the night as I broke through the front door of the club.

Blue drifts of smoke hung in the air under the shelter of the barn-like ceiling. I made my way around the wooden posts, waved hi to a few old-timers, and grabbed an open spot at the bar. It was still early. The Apollo's show hadn't let out, and that crowd had yet to arrive.

"Courvoisier, water back," I yelled above the noise to the bartender. Up and down the length of the room I saw groupings of heads—wooly and natural, processed, silky, braided, beaded, tied-and-dyed.

People hunched together, foreheads touching, voices raised in loud conversation. Laughter dived and swooped through the room. Words poured like clover honey out of people's mouths.

Black men drank, argued, exchanged easy lies, and occasionally jabbed chicken wings at one another to make a point. Sisters drank, cooed, and cajoled, loud-talked or screeched with laughter, and leaned in to their men like saplings bent into the wind.

I let the voices and the soul of all these black folk lift me. It was tonic to my spirit, like a Sunday morning hallelujah service. I surveyed the room once more, and that's when I saw her, sitting at the end of the bar. A tiny umbrella floated on top of her cherry-red drink.

I watched fascinated as she held the straw with her lips and maneuvered it past the umbrella and then sucked hard on it. The pull of her lips was long and slow, and my face heated up—beads of sweat popped out on my forehead as I watched. To the beat of the music, she dunked her straw up and down in the glass, and then she took another long pull. That's when I did something really stupid.

I ripped up my cocktail napkin, balled the pieces up, and flicked them at her. The same way I did in third grade to Hazel Fletcher across the cafeteria lunch table. At first the woman didn't notice the bits of paper being shot at her, and she continued to dunk her straw. Then, slowly, she raised her eyes in my direction and watched as I launched the last missile that landed smack in the middle of her drink.

Uh-oh. She arranged her brown velvet face into one of the most disapproving expressions I had ever seen, and plucked the paper out of the drink. And then, she sucked her teeth at me—her lips full, pouty and sexy. Think that discouraged me? No, like my aunt Reba used to say when I was young, I had a hard head and a soft behind.

Nothing had changed in thirty years. I still had a hard head, though my behind had gotten harder. At that moment, my hormones remembered their function, and at their urging I approached the woman.

She didn't acknowledge me as I slid my bulk into the space right next to her. I waited, smiled, and looked downright goofy. She cut her eyes at me and shifted her body away. A moment passed. Finally, the floodgates of heaven opened. She spoke.

"Only if you're single, have a job, a place to live, and haven't been locked up, then, *then* you can talk to me. Otherwise, don't, I'm warning you. Don't waste my time or yours."

Her voice rained over me like granulated sugar—gritty, but sweet. I looked up at the ceiling and reflected, then inclined my head toward her and said, "Would you go for one out of four?"

She stifled the smile that threatened to erupt from her face, turned to me, and began to swing a nicely shaped calf back and forth in my direction.

I was encouraged, eyes fixed on her calf. "That's a sign of sexual frustration, you know." Her leg stopped. Eyes rolled up into her head in disgust, and she turned back to the bar. She slurped noisily at her drink.

Probably the wrong thing to say.

"Let me buy you a drink. That one seems to be gone."

She continued to show me her back. I wasn't exactly displeased. It was a fine back. She had on some off-the-shoulder, off-the-back number, and I stood mesmerized, staring at her back and at each of her vertebrae. I was counting them when she turned back, scowling. This I thought to be a good sign, so I said, "Look, they let me out of the asylum one day a week. I'm rusty. The name is Amos, what's yours?" That smile she had been withholding spread slowly over her face, and she finally offered her hand. "Catherine."

Two fat dimples appeared on both sides of her cheeks. I was smitten. I took her hand in mine. I reacted without thinking. I looked at her hands. I said, "Damn, baby, you walk on these?"

Paralyzed for a second, she stared at me and then snatched her hand away. She was steaming, I could tell.

"I'm joking, just joking, that's all." I wasn't, but her rough hands caught me by surprise. I sputtered, "No, really, I like women with hands like yours. Makes you know they ain't afraid of hard work." And then I grabbed both of her hands in mine. "Look, these hands are tools. Made to build and create—civilizations and things—they're . . . they're great."

Now I thought I saw the steam blowing out from both sides of her head.

She said, "I think you should quit while you're behind."

Just as I was about to lay more of my sensitive rap on her I heard the hissing of a cobra next to my ear. Awwww, shit, no, it couldn't be. . . .

The rattle and hiss of asthmatic breathing made me turn. I was belly to belly with Harry the Monkey Chaser.

Wouldn't you know, in living color and stereophonic sound. Double shit. This wasn't Monday, and I wasn't prepared to talk to Harry. His muscle men, Blood Clots One and Two, stood shoulder to shoulder behind him.

"You botherin' this little lady here?" The lilt of Harry's West Indian accent swirled around my head like a small and deadly tornado.

Damn. A woman had just shot me down. Now I was going to get shot for real. This wasn't my day.

I adjusted my tie. "Harry, my man. Where you been?"

"Why you askin', Amos? You miss me?"

"Uh, sure . . ."

"Didn't know you cared. Visitin' the island. You know, Trinidad."

"Is that right? Heard it's beautiful this time of year."

"Enough chitty-chat, man. You got something for me? Me boys was looking for you, you know."

"And they didn't find me? Your fellows must have let down while you were gone, man." Harry's eyes closed into a slit. I didn't flinch, but my sphincter muscles bunched together.

"You got it on you?"

"Harry, I ain't stupid, man. Why would I carry that kind of money on me?"

"How 'bout just in case you be runnin' into me?"

Just as I was about to level with Harry, from behind me I heard, "Uncle Harry, why do you want to mess up the only date I've had in two months?"

I whipped my head around to look at Catherine. Harry also looked at Catherine. She looked up to me. I looked back at Harry. The three of us looked damned surprised.

Catherine said, "Amos was taking me out to a real nice dinner. I'm starved, aren't you, Aim?"

Aim? I deadpanned her and said, "Yeah, sure, ready when you are—uh, *Cath*."

Harry pushed past me and gave his niece a great hug and a resounding kiss on her cheek. "Me sweet-sweet. Didn't know you knew this man."

Catherine showed dimples to her uncle, then to me. She arranged a shawl about her shoulders, picked up her handbag, and said to me, "Ready?"

If I wasn't in love before, I was now. I took her arm and edged ever so carefully past Harry and his Blood Clots.

"Amos," Harry called. I tensed and stopped. He pulled a bill from his pocket and stuffed it into the breast pocket of my jacket. "Y'all have a good time, hear? Catherine is me only niece. But I ain't forgettin' nothin', you know. Be checking with you next week."

Stupefied, I kept my legs moving and waved to Harry. Outside, Catherine turned to me. "I love my uncle, but he has a bad habit. He kills people. I think he might have killed you."

I blew out breath I didn't realize I was holding. "I think you may be right. Looks like I owe you. Now what?" I looked into doe-brown eyes, soft from the glow of the moonlight.

She lifted the bill out of my pocket, glanced at it, and replaced it. "A hundred bucks? Looks like you're taking me to dinner." I smiled and we started to walk toward Baby when she suddenly stopped short in the middle of the street. What now?

"Wait, what's the one out of four?"

I waited a minute before answering, then I joked, "I got a place to live?"

Chapter 8

We dined at a place of her choosing, the Pink Teacup, located down in the East Village. The place didn't impress me much, but it made her happy. I couldn't complain. Harry was paying for it. We ordered some drinks.

"God, doesn't it feel good to get out of Harlem?" she said.

She didn't want to hear what I really thought, so I kept my mouth shut and asked her instead what she did for a living.

"Working as a nurse's aide now. At Columbia Presbyterian, the graveyard shift. I'm studying to be an R.N. and I go to school in the daytime." And then she paused.

"I moved back in with my mother five months ago. She had a heart attack, so you can forget about going back to my place. Amos, do you work?"

She was direct, I'll say that for her. She about blew my breath away. "Ah, the old West Indian work ethic, huh?" I smiled. "Who said anything about going back to your place?"

"Your eyes did. Do you work?"

Lucky it was my eyes she noticed, and not the little mind—I had been pushing it down all evening. "I . . . uh, own real estate. Sorry to hear about your mom."

"She's getting stronger. Did I hear you say you owned real estate?" Disbelief shimmered in her eyes.

I smiled again. "All black men don't lie."

The waiter chose that moment to set our drinks down. The air shifted between us. She reached for her drink while looking sideways at me and said, "Are you hooked up with my uncle?"

"Not by choice. I lost at poker. I bet more than my ass could cover. I owe Harry."

"God, that's a relief."

"Not to me. Harry's upset."

She looked down at the table and studied it. "I mean, it's a relief you're not hooked up selling drugs for Uncle Harry."

"You know about his drug business?"

She made a gesture with her hand. "Of course. He's my uncle—Harlem village is small. I love my uncle Harry. He's done a lot for me and my mom, but I don't like what . . ."

"I understand. Me either. Well, I'm surprised to be sitting here with his niece. Scared."

"Why? Not because I'm Harry's niece?"

"No, because you're you. That's enough to scare me."

Those dimples appeared in her cheeks, and she made a U-turn in the conversation.

"Tell me about you, Amos. You grew up in Harlem? Your parents live here?"

"Ah, you want the family tree. Okay. My mother, she died in childbirth in thirty-seven. I was raised by my dead mother's sister, Aunt Reba. Enough said."

"No, uh-uh, you can't stop there. You made an awful face just now. That wasn't a good thing?"

"To be raised by my aunt Reba?" My stomach churned acid at the memory of my childhood.

"My aunt Reba kept a roof over my head and gave me food to eat, and she fulfilled her obligation to her dead sister. Beyond that . . ." I chugalugged the rest of my drink and slammed the glass down on the table harder than I meant to.

"Uh-oh, stepped in some manure, didn't I? Something you don't want to talk about?"

"No, it's okay. This is the what's-your-sign-let's-get-acquainted part, huh? Let's get it over with. It should leave us that much more time for fun stuff later—at my place." I winked and tried to turn it into a joke. She didn't laugh.

"And your father?" she said.

Man, she was persistent. "I didn't know the man. I'd see him on the street sometimes, but the only time I had any real contact with him was one time when I was twelve and Aunt Reba called him to come discipline me." Catherine waited for me to go on. "He took a bat to me, broke my jaw, and I promised not to steal anymore. I didn't hear from him until I was grown. He only lived four blocks away, but you know, that's the way it is in Harlem."

"Yeah, I know," she said. "Your world is your block, especially when you're a kid. Shoot, that's why I want to get out now—Harlem suffocates. It wraps itself around you and won't let you go. I'm dying here."

Puzzled, I looked at her to see if she was kidding. I said, "Harlem is what I'm used to. It's home to me. Besides, I can't think of anyplace else I'd rather be."

"You're in a box, Amos, and you're all tied up. There's a world of possibilities outside of Harlem, you know."

The way she moved the word *Harlem* around in her mouth grated on me, but I didn't argue with her. Catherine kept looking at me, and after a pause, I went on with my story.

"Anyway, after the bat, I'd hear about my father and his goings-on—his women, his drinking, and big-timing, and he'd hear about me, my fighting, thieving, and trouble-making, but we were both glad to steer clear of one another. My aunt was more than overjoyed when the police picked me up and deposited me in a state prison. She probably dusted her hands together and said, "Good riddance." Hell, I don't blame the woman. I was sullen, angry, and nobody's child. I wouldn't have wanted to raise me either."

I saw disappointment register in Catherine's eyes. "Jail?" she said.

I gently reminded her. "One out of four, remember. Yeah, a state prison, which I have to admit did a superb job of raising me. I had an intensive life course, and I learned my lessons well. When I was twenty they drop-kicked my ass out of there."

"Why were you . . . ?"

"You don't want to know," I said.

"Oh," she answered.

Our dinner arrived, and after that we ate in silence. I chewed over more than my food, and I'm sure she did, too. I hated to admit that our first date wasn't much of a success. Mr. Smooth here turned out to be too big of a lump for Catherine to swallow. Well hell, I wasn't used to lying. She fell asleep over dessert, and I took her home.

At her doorstep, she apologized for falling asleep and blamed it on her schedule. I tried to make her feel better by not disagreeing with her. And then, the oddest thing, she asked me for my phone number.

It wasn't until I jumped into Baby parked at the curb that I realized that I was supposed to ask for *her* phone number. Oh well, Mr. Smooth. I flipped on the tape deck. Okay Sam, me and you. Sing it, bro', sing it—

"*. . . a cha-a-nge is gonna come . . .*"

Chapter 9

Monday morning I kept my promise to Patty and took her to the Social Services office. What a zoo. I ended up cussing out three orangutan clerks and one social caseworker, species unknown. From the size of her overbite I suspected she descended from a vicious breed of rodent.

I became convinced of it after she accused me, out of the blue, of being the father of Patty's child. Without so much as a by-your-leave, she pushed some papers at me to fill out. I explained to her as rationally as I could the error of her thinking. She shoved the papers at me again and gave me an ultimatum. Pissed me off big time. I told her where she could stick her papers and watched as she ground her horse teeth together while the veins in her Cro-Magnon cranium popped and slithered like snakes across her wide forehead. Still, I was cool, until she started screeching at me like a hyena and called for security.

Then I lost it. Me and her went at it, tit for tat, bony for fat.

I talked about the social welfare system and included her mama. She called me a scum-of-the-earth pig who didn't have a mama. I called her a buck-toothed-bitch-in-heat-who-wished-she-could-snag-a-man-so-she-could-*be*-a mama. It went on like that for a while. Patty didn't say a word and stood trembling beside me. I kept propping her up so she wouldn't disappear through the cracks in the floor.

Well, don't you know, a crowd gathered. People cheered and jeered. Soon the entire fifth floor of the Social Services office building was in an uproar. An old woman leaning on a walker attached herself to me and bounced her walker up and down with glee at all the commotion. Out of the corner of my eye I saw three rent-a-cops rush toward me, but two beefy brothers with linebacker shoulders stopped them dead in their tracks.

A supervisor type, and a Barney Rubble look-alike, flew out of his office, and elbowed his way through the crowd. I'll give him this—Barney-boy tried to calm things down, but the social worker wouldn't stop shrieking. Truth be told, I was going pretty good too.

Barney's head revolved like the door at the Waldorf-Astoria as he simultaneously attempted crowd control and made an effort to hush the two of us up. He tsk-tsked and tut-tutted in all the right places, as he managed at last to herd the three of us into his office and shut the door.

Above the continuing tirade of the caseworker, I explained things to Barney, best as I was able. He finally suggested that Bertha (that was her name) take a break. She turned zit red and spat out something about male chauvinist pigs who stuck together, and huffed off.

A welcome silence billowed through the office. Barney smiled. We bonded. He assured me that all he wanted to do was avoid a Monday morning riot. "That wasn't asking too much, was it?" he said. He asked what it would take to make me happy. I told him what I wanted. The man was righteous.

Patty had a check in her hand when we left the office. We waved to the crowd and even got a few high fives.

That done, it was time to think about me. I had a decision to make. I dropped Patty off at the hospital again and made my way home—by way of New Jersey. The long drive settled me and gave me time to think. I slipped in a Miles Davis tape and chilled. By the time I pulled up in front of home-sweet-home a couple of hours later, I knew what I had to do. Could I do it? That was the question.

I stroked Baby's leather-covered steering wheel one last time and sprang from the car, prepared to TCB—take care of business. When I made my mind up to do something, I did it.

Hold that thought, and later for the business. Across the street I saw cops swarming like maggots in front of my other brownstone. I recognized Detectives Bundt and Caporelli. They were shooting the shit on the front stoop, smoking cigarettes, while six police techs busted their butts to heft a large tarp-bundled object into the rear of a waiting police van. Another cop stripped yellow tape from the premises while the rest of the boys in blue loaded odd items of police paraphernalia, carpenters' tools, picks, and shovels into radio cars. Seltzer was smack in the middle of them, getting in the way. I signaled to him, and he ambled over.

"Look like you back in business, boss."

"You think?"

"Sure. Cops are leaving. Won't see them fellows no more. Oh, uh, before I forget, a guy come by looking for you. Must've known something. Asked about renting the basement front." He shoved a scrap of paper at me with a phone number on it.

"He know about the skeleton?"

Seltzer made a raspberry with his lips. "He don't give a rat's ass. What he care about some skeleton?"

"Some people . . . superstition, you know."

"What somebodies you talking about? Yourself?"

I slipped the paper into my shirt pocket and avoided his question. "I'll take care of it. How's the back apartment look? How big a hole we got?"

The cop cars pulled off, and I stopped and waved good-bye. Sure as hell going to miss them.

"Well, the hole ain't the size of Texas, but it ain't no Rhode Island neither. Maybe Tennessee, I reckon."

I shuffled my feet. Seltzer's version of geography wasn't what I wanted to hear, and I cut to the chase. "How much?"

"Got to replace a four-by-twelve, plaster, paint . . . Don't worry, I can do the job cheap."

"You sure? Because this bank"—and I pointed to myself—"has run dry."

I passed him a credit card that was legit, from one of those financial institutions that pushed it on people with homeowner status, but which I had never used.

See, everything I ever bought was always cash money. You didn't do street transactions with a credit card. So I had no use for credit rip-offs. If there was one thing I was good at, it was math, and I sure as hell could compute interest. The bank vig was higher than the vig on the street. It didn't take no genius to figure that out. If you ask me, credit wasn't nothing but legalized thievery from poor folks who don't know no better. I sure as hell knew better, but desperate times . . .

"Here," I said to Seltzer. "Use it for supplies. I trust you. Get it back to me tomorrow."

Seltzer pushed the card away. "What's that? I don't want nothing to do with no writing. Looky here, I'll tell you what you need and you can pick up the dang supplies yourself. That way, won't be no problem."

I smiled. Seltzer wasn't fooling nobody, but you had to understand him. He was no different from the brothers I had done time with. Stuck in that middle passage—street-wise, dog-smart, but not able to read, and not able to make the jump to opportunity.

Take Slew-Foot Reggie for example, an ex-con and numbers runner, able to carry hundreds of numbers around in his head, but couldn't fill out a job application if his life depended on it. One thing I did, I put my time to good use in the joint—got the equivalent of a college education with all the books I devoured. Reading was the one thing that motivated me to finally get wise, and stay out of solitary confinement—because, hell, in solitary, the guards wouldn't let you read.

Well, maybe you could read the Bible. Read it from cover to cover, and back again. Not because I was a believer, but because it was there, although I've always had a healthy respect for things I didn't understand. But I guess that tells you how many times they had my ass in solitary. I knew the Bible well.

My man Seltzer was smart in his own way, talented too, and I recognized his talent, but I couldn't give the cat the satisfaction of knowing it. Damn straight, what's the fun of that? So I called him a no-good trifling blankety-blank, too lazy to pick up some piddling supplies. I said, "Make a list and give it to me."

He frothed. "Make the list your own damn self."

"What? I got to do everything? You got a tree stump for a brain?"

He bristled and bucked and said at least he had a brain. What was my excuse? I laughed. My buddy. I could count on Seltzer. Exchanging insults made us both feel good. Cleansed somehow. Not like with the social worker. Thinking about her gave me hives.

"Well," I said as Seltzer stood waiting, "don't you have something to do? Admiring my good looks ain't what I'm paying you for, so get to stepping."

Seltzer hoisted his balls at me, told me to kiss his black ass, and went back to work. I chuckled and watched him go.

From behind me I heard the tip-tapping of a cane coming down the brownstone's steps, and turned to see Mr. Evil himself.

"Hey, Zeke. Need a few words with you," I said.

Zeke hurriedly shoved open the low iron gate with his cane, spoke not a word to me, and took off in the direction of Sixth Avenue as fast as his spindly legs could carry him.

I watched his retreat and shook my head. I wasn't made of the stuff to chase an old man down the street. But I was going to make it a point to corner his narrow butt tomorrow and squeeze rent out of him, or begin eviction proceedings. I inwardly shuddered at the paperwork involved. But that was my job now—landlord.

Well, first things first. I walked through the gate and paused by the tree that still bugged the shit out of me. The words NIGGER LANDLORD were still recognizable on the tree trunk. Seltzer hadn't been able to make them disappear. He whitewashed over the letters, but the fluorescence of the paint bled through. And if that weren't enough, the oak's roots had given me the finger by buckling the concrete leading up to my stoop—another something to take care of.

A summer breeze lifted a branch of the tree, and a tentacle of the old oak scratched my cheek. Did that tree talk back to me?

Huh. I touched my cheek. Superstitious? Maybe Seltzer was right. I barked at the tree as I mounted the steps. "Screw you, too," I said.

In the same moment, Wilbur came out of the door and ran smack into me. "Ooh, Mr. Brown, I heard that. Was that an invitation or a promise?" he said.

"Easy, Wilbur, easy." I stepped back and gave him a wide berth. Today Wilbur was not subtle. He had on a purple and scarlet outfit, with a fringed purple scarf, and wore platform-heeled shoes as high as a woman's. Under one arm, he carried a teddy bear with a big red bow.

"Hi-hi, Mr. Brown."

I sighed. Every day Wilbur tested my tolerance level. Today I thought seriously about throwing him over the railing.

"One 'Hi' is plenty, Wilbur." I raised my eyebrows at the bear cuddled in his arms. He noticed.

"Oh, this? This is Buddy Bear. Isn't he sweet? I'm taking it to Josie in the hospital."

Okay, so I didn't toss him. I informed him that I had dropped Patty off at the hospital a couple of hours ago.

He asked, "Did they find out what's wrong with little Josie?"

"Suspect malnutrition. Running more tests to make sure."

"That doesn't sound right."

"What doesn't sound right?"

"Malnutrition. Patty would go without food herself so she could feed that baby. She took good care of Josie, I know she did. You think she's going to be all right, Mr. B.?"

"We'll find out soon enough. Don't worry, Wilbur. The baby is in good hands."

"Winnie upstairs? She was always giving that baby food. Me too. Couldn't be malnutrition. No, no, Mr. B."

"Okay, okay, Wilbur . . . give it a rest. The doctors will find out."

"I'm taking myself over there right this minute. It pains me to know Josephine's in that hospital all by herself."

"Patty's there, Wilbur."

"Well, I know that, but we're family in this building. All of us except, uh, you know."

"Zeke?"

"Child, you hit it, but you ain't heard it from these lips."

Which translated into Wilbur's being ready to spill all. "What's Zeke's problem?"

"Well . . ."

I waited. Wilbur was primed.

"See, at first when I moved in, I thought it was just me, 'cause you know, but no—Zeke hates everybody. Maybe the man was disappointed in love."

On "love" Wilbur batted his eyes and placed a hand over his heart. My own eyebrows shifted a notch higher.

"But when you took over the building, he got really testy—agitated, you know. Between you and me, I know it was him who did *that*." Wilbur pointed to the tree. My eyebrows stretched to my hairline and I exploded.

"You saw him?"

"Not exactly, but that same paint stayed right there in the hallway outside his door for two whole weeks. It sure didn't belong to me. I guess you missed it."

True, I hadn't made the climb to the third floor in those first few weeks after I took over the building.

"What burr does Zeke have up his butt about me?"

"Child, don't get me to lying. I don't have a clue. You don't know?"

Wilbur leaned forward and waited for a gossipy tidbit to drop in his ear. It wasn't going to happen. I stood my ground. Wilbur sighed, and moved to the next subject.

"Oh, Mr. B., did I tell you I baked an apple pie?"

"That right?"

"Uh-huh. If you like . . ." And then Wilbur's voice plummeted an octave, and he winked. "If you like," he repeated, "I'll drop you off a piece."

I leaped backward, horrified. My face got hot. Wilbur chortled.

"Talking about *pie*, Mr. B. See ya." Flinging his scarf over one shoulder, he laughed again and flounced down the steps.

Wilbur was pulling my chain, I knew it. I unlocked the door to my office. Damn hermaphrodite. But hell, the man could burn. No lie. That I could testify to. I looked forward to his pie.

I entered the office, plopped into my swivel chair, let my head fall back, and stared for a time at the ceiling. A water stain stared back at me. God, it was only Monday. I let out a sigh; then I summoned the will and pitched forward and rifled through the Rolodex on my desk and pulled out a card with Herman Brubaker's name on it, a Cadillac dealer I had been doing business with for the past ten years.

I reached for the phone and suddenly choked—this was going to be damn hard. I sat for a full minute, receiver in hand, dial tone insistent and vibrating through my fingers. Overhead, Winnie's stereo played; the bass boomed and the ceiling pulsed in rhythm to the thumping of my heart. *Courage*, I said, and dialed Herman's number.

Herman picked up on the second ring. Over the wires I heard him stuff his gut, lips smacking. Can there be a more disgusting sound than a human sucking on a bone? I cut short his description of what he was eating and got to the point.

"Herman? Unloading my car. What'll you give me for it?" I waited until his coughing and hacking subsided, and asked again. Since it wasn't my usual trade up, he hem-hawed before he gave me a figure.

When I heard it I demanded to know what fool in what universe he thought he was talking to. I told the scuzz I'd be at his car lot in thirty minutes and left him with, "Eat your chicken before I get there, Herman, or I'll stuff it down your greedy throat and you'll really choke."

Satisfied with my finesse and persuasive skills, I slammed down the receiver, leaned back in my chair, fingers laced behind my head. See, when you argue with a man—everything's simple.

Chapter 10

The phone was ringing off the hook in my apartment as I entered my bedroom and threw myself across the bed. I let it ring and squirreled my body deeper into the covers. I was depressed. The money for Harry now burned a hole in my pocket and I could smell the smoke. I lay face down, and began a purple dream. I was in a poker game. The cards and chips levitated and flew through the air. Harry was furious with me. He pulled out a bottle of rum from underneath the table and chased me across the George Washington Bridge, the bottle of rum in one hand, and a shot glass in the other, screaming at the top of his lungs. I was terrified. It must have been rush hour because cars were stalled bumper to bumper across the length of the bridge. I jumped in and out of successive cars, tried to start their engines, and not one turned over. Grilles upturned in smiles, the cars laughed. I was desperate.

Catherine balanced on a railing, about to take a flying leap off the bridge, but I couldn't save her. Even as she called to me—Harry was closing in. Then Catherine morphed into the buck-toothed social worker and jumped from the bridge, her body spiraling down into a churning Hudson River.

I sprang awake to the phone ringing and Catherine's name on my lips. I rubbed my eyes. All the lights were on. I looked at the clock on the nightstand. Nine o'clock. I was confused. Was it morning or night? The phone continued to ring. I snatched it from its cradle.

"Hi," the voice said.

"Okay," I said.

"What kind of way is that to answer a phone? Were you sleeping?"

"No, of course not. I, uh, was watching television." Why did I lie? Why do people lie when they're caught sleeping? I still wasn't sure if it was day or night. While I made an effort to unfog my brain, wouldn't you know, Catherine asked me what program I was watching.

"*Bonanza*," I said. "Why are you calling me?"

"Amos, that's a dumb question. You don't want me to call you? Is that what you're saying?"

"Of course I want you to call me. I just don't know why you're calling me. I didn't think you would call. I'm not used to women calling me."

Silence on the line. "Is this a line you're pulling on me, Amos?"

I didn't know what she was talking about, but I laughed and said, "Ha, you caught me." Then I heard another long pause, and I wondered what I was supposed to say.

Catherine helped me out. She said, "I think it would be a good idea if we went on another date."

I sat up in bed. I was wide-awake now. "Exactly what I was thinking, but you beat me to it."

Another silence. "Amos, are you *sure* you're awake?"

I rubbed my eyes and slapped my face and said, "Look, maybe we could go to a club, some place downtown, even."

"I was thinking of a movie."

"Better. What day and time?"

"Sunday's my only day off. Let's make it afternoon, if that's all right with you. Pick me up at three?"

"Three's good. Hey." I paused for effect and gave her full baritone. "I was thinking about you." It wasn't exactly a lie. I had just had a nightmare and she was in it. I heard her soft voice answer, "I've been thinking about you too."

I couldn't think of anything else to say, so I said, "I'll be counting the days until Sunday."

I heard her smile through the phone. Well, I imagined I heard her smile, but actually, she was cracking up, way loud.

She said, "Good-bye, Amos."

I hung up. Oh yeah, now I was thinking about her. I'd probably be thinking about her all week. Well, shit. That was when I remembered I had no wheels. Baby was sitting on the northwest corner of Herman's car lot with a for-sale sign splayed across her windshield. I fell back on the bed. Between now and Sunday, I'd come up with something.

Tomorrow I'd go by Harry's and pay him. I pulled the covers over my head and tried to sleep. Didn't work, so I stayed up to read a worn copy of *David Copperfield* and pushed to the happy ending.

Chapter 11

The next morning, the sky clouded over and drops of rain plunked a mournful tune against the windows in my office. A good day to stay in bed, but I had things to do and Harry to see. Yet here I was, sitting at my desk, drinking burnt coffee just waiting for heartburn. I was also waiting for the electrician downstairs to finish up.

Don't you know, sometime during the night the electricity went.

Bleary-eyed, I awoke to Winnie banging on my apartment door. I answered the door in my boxers—the ones with the loose elastic. It didn't dawn on me until Winnie blushed brown that I was an eighth of an inch away from exposing myself. But it didn't stop her from gabbing at length and in great detail about the problem with the electricity. Since she handed me a home-baked muffin, warm from the oven, I silently forgave her for the flagrant violation of the office hour rule I had posted on my door just yesterday.

What the hell—the newest tenant in number 1, George, didn't respect my sign either. He pounded on my door right after Winnie left, and handed me nothing but a lot of lip.

You would think that a grown man who worked on the trucks for the Sanitation Department could deal with a little inconvenience. Instead, George threw a hissy fit that would make even Wilbur sit up and take notice. He trooped upstairs from his basement apartment three times, bothering me. Now tell me, was it my fault that he was late for work? Did I blow the damn fuses? The last thing on earth I wanted was for any tenant of mine to miss a day's work. Not me. And jeopardize their ability to pay me my rent? Hell no. I gave him a flashlight and told him to use it where it would do the most good.

Seltzer put in new fuses, but it didn't do any good. Each time he replaced them, they blew. After the third blowout I was forced to call an electrician. He arrived three hours later and I escorted him to the cellar, where he played blind man's bluff with Seltzer. They didn't need me, so I came on upstairs.

And now I was sitting in my swivel chair, doing what I was supposed to do. Hell, I swiveled. And slugged orange juice—drops of which now dribbled down my chin. Great. I thought about today's agenda. What lay ahead left me in a funk—as funky as the weather outside my window.

I turned once again to look at the gloom, when wouldn't you know it, the sun broke through a stormy cloud—the devil was kissing his wife—and light radiated through the room and danced through the prisms of my empty juice glass. Rainbows of light cavorted across the notes hung to the bulletin board on the wall above my desk. I watched the light as it played across the paper, and then I noticed the forgotten scrap of paper with a name and number scrawled across it, winking eyeball height in front of me.

Oh yeah, the paper that Seltzer had handed me yesterday. Okay, a sign for me to call this joker. I snatched the paper off the board. The thumbtack that held it zapped me on the chin and rolled under the desk. Was that another sign?

While I scrounged on the floor looking for the tack I thought, okay, if I could rent out another apartment, maybe I'd come out in the black this month. The tack stabbed me in the hand; I retrieved it, then bumped my head on the desk as I got up. See? I knew I should have stayed in bed. What was the saying? If it wasn't for bad luck, I wouldn't have no luck at all.

I dialed the phone. No answer. It rang fourteen times. Disgusted, I hung up and made the call I'd been putting off. I called Harry. It was near noon, about time for him to crawl out from under his rock. Lucky me—Harry picked up on the first ring.

"Harry? Amos here. Got your money. Be around this afternoon?"

It was difficult to understand Harry because he was wheezing heavy. Between wheezes he told me to meet him at his pool hall, his official place of business, around three. Wheeze or no wheeze, Harry also let me know in no uncertain terms that it was a good thing I called him, before he had to call me.

The sound of my front doorbell ringing interrupted the conversation, and I was happy for an excuse to terminate my call to Harry.

"Harry, my man, glad you're glad. Got to take care of some urgent business. Later." I caught myself before I slammed down the phone. With two hands I eased the receiver into its cradle. No need to upset Harry unnecessarily.

That done, I peered through my office window. In the rain, on the stoop, stood a tall, skinny wimp hefting a blasting radio on his shoulder that rattled my windows. What now?

He jabbed his finger repeatedly on the bell. I shot out of my office and wrenched the front door open.

"What do you want?" I yelled, over the disco beat that pumped out of his booming box.

"You Amos Brown?"

"Yeah."

"Left a note for you yesterday."

"Yeah?"

"About renting the basement apartment across the street."

I frowned and indicated his radio. "Turn that damn thing off before you electrocute yourself."

Youngblood itched to jump bad with me, but thought better of it and clicked the radio off, his lips poked out.

Jesus, the kid's music was not even good R&B.

Youngblood wiped the water that hung off the tip of his nose and said, "Uh, look, man," he said, "it's raining out here."

Like this was news to me.

I held the door open and pointed him to my office. Asshole didn't bother to stamp the water off of his feet, and left a wet trail on the carpeted hallway.

Young fool hadn't stepped one foot good inside the door before he asked, "How about it?"

I looked at him like he was crazy. "How about what?" I said.

"Renting the apartment."

I told him to slow his roll and take a load off. Then I sat in my chair while I inspected him from head to foot. A little too slick for my taste. Long sideburns and a nickel's worth of goatee adorned his face. His pants hung low on his hips, and he wore sissy high-heeled white patent leather shoes that covered the boats he used for feet. Strung about his neck were a couple of gold chains of the clunky variety.

The water puddled at his feet. I shrugged off my irritation and asked him, "What do you do for a living?"

"Uh . . . student," he said.

The pause between "uh" and "student" registered. And his eyes darted to the left. Hmph. Kid had some con going, I'd bet on it.

"Rent's three hundred fifty a month," I said.

"No problem. Got a part-time job, and, uh, a scholarship."

Lying his ass off. God, was this me, at his age? I hoped not. I pointed to his radio. "I got working people living in the building. You play that thing all the time?"

"Ah, naw, naw, man. Just, you know, sometimes."

I gave him the once-over again.

He stretched his lanky body to put a hand into the pocket of his tight pants and extracted a wad of bills. Holy shit, twice the size of the roll that had a current home in my pocket. I resisted comment as he counted off ten one-hundred-dollar bills and offered them to me.

"Ain't got no recommendation, but I can give you three months' rent plus a deposit," he said. "See, where I'm staying, ain't a good situation. Need to move somewheres right away."

I hesitated. "College boy, huh? Who says 'ain't'? Well, sonny boy, that'll be *three* months' rent, *plus* a deposit and a cleaning fee, which comes to sixteen hundred even. Can you handle that?" I smiled at him.

He smiled back, real cocky, and said, "No problem, Pops, and shit, 'ain't' is good English where I come from."

Thirty-eight years old, and he's calling me "Pops"? It took as much as I could muster not to knock all the black off of him.

I asked instead, "Where you from, Youngblood?"

"D.C., man."

He peeled six bills off his roll and pushed them at me. I blinked. Though I wouldn't go so far as to say I snatched the money, the money passed from him to me in a definite blur, and I crammed the bills deep in my shirt pocket. You would've thought I was a magician, I moved so fast.

Then I unswiveled myself from my chair and retrieved the keys to the apartment from a hook on the wall. "Basement front is ready to go. Move in today if you want."

I whipped out a lease from the bottom desk drawer and he signed it. Grabbed his hand, pumped it, and made him listen to my short speech about respecting the other tenants and the neighbors. I ended with a stern "Don't shit where you live," and crunched his skinny fingers between mine to make the point. He flinched, the pain evident, and agreed to every word out of my mouth.

Meanwhile Patty had tiptoed down from upstairs and stuck her head in the door and said, "Mr. Brown? You busy?"

"No, Patty, just finishing up business," I said. "Come on in." I noticed Youngblood's eyes light up and skim over Patty's body. I introduced them and Patty blushed. Then she crept into the room and pushed the blood red purse at me. Youngblood jumped back, eyes bucking.

"Ain't right for Josie. She be eating the rocks and stuffing the feathers in her mouth, so I'm giving it back, okay?"

I took the purse from her. "Sure, I understand—should have thought of that myself." Patty smiled, slithered around the wall, ducked out of the room, and went back up the stairs. Youngblood and I watched her go.

Youngblood turned to me and said, "You know what that is? You'd better get rid of that shit. That's voodoo mess, Jack."

"Yeah?" I looked at him and down at the purse, and felt my face grow warm. Shock, then a flush of understanding swept over me. A tremor, and I thought of Josie. I was steamed and with good reason. Zeke—damn his eyes. Had to be. To Youngblood I said, "Name's Amos—and don't forget it."

Then I handed him the keys to his new apartment and pointed

him across the street to my other brownstone. Told him I'd catch up with him in a minute. With one hand I waved him out of the room and dialed Herman's number with the other.

While I waited for Herman to pick up, I fiddled with the bag and wondered what kind of vermin I had under my roof. Zeke and his shenanigans. The tree and now this.

Me, I never believed in that superstitious shit . . . just didn't like to see coincidences collide. It did make you wonder—Josie's illness . . . Naw, I dismissed the thought as unworthy, but grew hot again at the idea that Zeke would bring that foolishness around here, trying to put a hex on me. I had reached my boiling point and when I caught up with Zeke, he was about to get scalded.

I blew like a stallion and whacked the phone against the desk. What was taking Herman so long? And then I wondered. What kind of decent ride could I get for sixteen hundred bucks.

Chapter 12

No sooner had I finished talking to Herman than here she came, tipping up the front steps, shielded from the rain by a large umbrella, in all her paid-for-by-me finery. Gloria—I knew it was her. Must have sniffed the money. I took the money out of my shirt pocket, clipped it, and transferred it to my pants.

Gorgeous Gloria. There have been times in my life when I considered myself to be certifiable—and my time with Gloria was one of those insane times. At a crossroads, I thought wife, home, and family were what I needed. I made a mistake with Gloria. She wasn't about to have a crumb-snatcher, it'd ruin her figure, she said, and pitched a bitch when I quit the numbers and the cash flow dried up. She had worked up to a cocaine habit that had gotten out of hand. A little bit of blow now and then had turned into a lot of blow—almost every night, it seemed.

I avoided home and her, and she avoided me—packed and went right out the door, taking every valuable thing she could lay her hands on. Me, I didn't care. Tell the truth, I was glad to get rid of her. At any price. Well, here she was again.

She rang the bell. I resigned myself and answered it. After all, we did have unfinished business. Her peepers opened wide at the sight of me, and a practiced tear slid down one of her cheeks.

"Amos," she said, and threw her arms around my neck. Her perfume tempted me—almost. I slid her arms from around my neck and led the way to my office. No need to play this scene out on the front steps. The neighbors knew enough about me as it was. I didn't need to give them more fodder.

Gloria entered the office and glanced around, then slid one hand over her rump in that way she had, pelvis thrust forward, and waited for me—to what? To embrace her?

"Take a load off, Gloria." And I offered her a seat.

She smiled. "How's tricks, Amos?"

"Tricks?" I said. "I don't know, Gloria. Tricks is more your speed." That set her off.

"What are you talking about? I never tricked a day in my life, and you know it."

"Yeah? What did you call our relationship?" I said.

Her eyes snapped. She refused to respond to that, but said instead, "I need some money."

I chuckled. "See?"

"I ain't tricking. We're still married and I need some money."

"Well, good luck in getting it. You came to the wrong person."

"You look like you're doing okay."

"You do, too. Looks can be deceiving, now, can't they?"

"Amos, look, I ain't playing. They about to put me out where I'm staying."

"Where you staying?" I asked.

"Upper West Side, Eighty-second and Amsterdam."

I raised my eyebrows. "Pricey neighborhood."

She bowed her head and fumbled with her fingers. "My friend Marvin—he put me up."

A shock of recognition. Marvin the Gimp, I'd bet. Mafioso underdog, a non-Italian, but tied in deep with the mob. Hung out in all the black joints, loved him some black pussy. So he got next to my wife. Slimy motherfucker.

"Huh . . . you talking about Marvin the Gimp?"

Gloria nodded, started sniveling, and fat tears plopped down on her lap.

"Put you up. Now he's put you out, is that the way it goes?"

Gloria bobbed her head in short jerks like a puppet and sobbed.

I sighed and paused for a long and weighted moment. Her sobs got louder. Finally I said, "Got an apartment across the way you can stay in. For a month—only a month, understand? No money, I ain't got it. But I'll give you a place to stay until you get back on your feet." And even while I said it, I peeled off a hundred from my money clip and gave it to her. Her eyes bugged at the cash I held in my hand.

"This ain't mine. Don't get your hopes up—I'm giving it to someone soon's I finish with you." I handed her the keys to number 6 across the street, the apartment next to Miss Ellie. I regretted my decision as soon as I made it. But what could I do? I was a sucker. So what else was new?

Gloria tried to leap into my arms, but I sidestepped her and she bumped into the dresser. I reached for my hat and a jacket. "And I'll pay for the divorce lawyer—get one."

That cooled her motor. She took a step back and gave me the once-over, like she knew I couldn't be serious, and slid her hands down her hips again. I ignored her, showed her across the street to the apartment, settled her and Youngblood, and took off for Harry's.

Yeah, so okay, so maybe I had to tuck my bone back down my pants. What the fuck. It had a mind of its own, no matter what I thought.

The wind kicked up on the way to Harry's, but I was cool.

Chapter 13

I hiked up Seventh Avenue to 136th Street. Even though the shortest distance between two points is a straight line, I took the scenic route to Harry's. The walk lightened my mood and I began to groove with it. Even when my right sock crept into my shoe. Even when my heel began to hurt. Truth be told, I hadn't walked these streets in a great while. I ignored the chill in the June air as the wind nipped at me and the rain drizzled down. Summertime, children, and the weather was strange.

The wind played "tag, you're it" with my chapeau, and I pulled it down tight on my head. Like any tourist I checked out Harlem with new eyes. Okay, could be I was dragging my butt because I wasn't in a great hurry to turn over all this dough to Harry, so any diversion was a good excuse, but no lie, I marveled at Harlem's architecture.

For a ghetto, Harlem had amazing buildings. I had heard the term neoclassicism before, and that sounded about right. Heard it from old Charlie Caldwell, a friend and one of the few dudes I knew who had escaped these mean streets and made it through college. With a degree in architecture no less. God, hadn't thought about him in years. Charlie lived over in Jersey now, Teaneck. Too bad no one ever let him design a house. Doing drafting, last I heard.

Equal opportunity? Nope. Not for a black man. Not yet. And people wonder why so many black men take to the streets. Ain't waiting for some white man's by-your-leave, that's why. Independence. Bicentennial celebration notwithstanding—a separate case for a separate race. A wave washed over me. Well, at least Charlie escaped this hustle.

My heels dug into the pavement and I kept a steady pace. Voices jangled past my ears and fell like meteorites around me. Other voices, sweet and melodic, purred greetings in the familiar yo, sister-girl, brother-man, baby, sucker, sugar, honey, mama, daddy, niggah, my *main* man—the list endless.

Across the street, hanging from the window on the second story of a turn-of-the-century building, cigarette dangling loosely between lips, and melon breasts propped upon a window pane, a fleshy Nefertiti, head wrapped in a colorful scarf, threw coins down and shouted instructions to a child standing on the street below. A portrait, framed by stone ornamental moldings and sculpted bas-relief, telling in its rendering.

More people than a little bit lived in sumptuous Harlem digs. The poorest families often resided in brownstones and apartment buildings with high ceilings, crown molding, marbled foyers and fireplaces, dumbwaiters, crafted staircases, built-in bookcases, desks and doors made of mellowed antique wood. Of course their digs might be the worse for wear inside, but still . . .

I smiled. Wait until white people remembered what they gave up. Ooowee. New York was busting out at the seams. Couldn't wait for the stampede.

Harry's combo bar/office and pool hall was the second building from the corner on the west side of the street. I crossed over, paused, and looked back down the avenue that used to be a promenade of sorts during the twenties and thirties and shook my head.

Towering trees still lined the street, and rain misted their leaves. Uptown from Central Park, here was an oasis in a teeming city. In Harlem's heydey, men and women strolled this street on a Sunday afternoon dressed in all their finery.

Seeing the street jigged a memory. When I was nine, black servicemen, home from the war, marched along this very same avenue. This little black biscuit shoved and pushed his face in between sweaty, excited bodies to get a better view. I stood among the tens of thousands of black folk who lined the sidewalks, waving flags.

People cheered and cried. The fact that they cried mystified me then. Almost forty years later, I understood.

I swept the expanse of street with my eyes and despaired at its deterioration. When I turned back to continue on to Harry's, a drunk came out of nowhere and lurched across my path. He plowed headfirst into a tree and yelped and sucked air like he was about to pop a load. Didn't miss a beat, I kept on trucking and at 136th Street I crossed over and came to a stop beside the filigreed iron doors that fronted Harry's place.

The lookout man pressed his remote, a signal to Harry inside, and nodded me in. I entered the dim interior of the bar. The stale odor of beer and cigarettes drifted up my nostrils. It had been two months since I had stepped foot in Harry's, and as far as I could tell, no one in the bar had changed positions—the same bunch of fellows hung out. Astounding to me that time had stood still in this place, while my life had moved like a whirlwind.

At the far end of the room a familiar figure sat, tucked away into a corner table. I did a double take. Shit-head Zeke, what was he doing here? The connection fell into place. He and Harry were countrymen—Trinidadians.

I slapped hands all around with the rest of the bloods, and kept one eye out for Zeke. No way was he escaping this time. Deacon Steadwell, him I pounded and gripped in a bear hug.

Steadwell I had known forever. If I ever had such a thing as a mentor, Steadwell would be it. The man was old when I was a kid, and he remained unchanged. Going strong, after forty years on the street. Where the action was, that's where you found Steadwell—a clever hustler and booster. Far as I knew, Steadwell never went in for no gangster stuff, unlike the rest of the people that hung out in Harry's. Everybody liked having him around. Always quick with a joke and he listened when you talked to him.

Place an order with Steadwell, count on it. He would come up with whatever merchandise you wanted, no matter the size, shape, or weight. It was a wonder how he did it.

His lean body stretched across the green felt of the pool table. He held his cue stick between arthritic fingers and struggled with his aim. I asked him how he was doing.

"Same-o, same-o," he replied. "Deacon is still freaking, Skids over there still smells funky, and the rest of the cats here still crying the blues about life, the lack of liberty, and the pursuit of pussy. In there!" he said as he slammed the five ball into the corner pocket, his body following after.

"Hold on there, old-timer." And I helped him off the table.

Steadwell pushed himself upright with more than a little difficulty. "Ain't seen you around, Amos. What I heard true, you the heir to a Harlem kingdom? Moving up in the world, boy?"

"Sideways, Steadwell, moving sideways. You seen Harry?"

"He in the back. Guess you be joining one of them lodges, huh, Amos? Guess you be buying one of them BMWs now?"

I laughed. This Harlem heir business had moved me a step down in the world. I made the good money when I banked numbers. Raw from the walk, my heel attested to the fact. The status symbol I best represented and my only mode of transportation at the moment was not BMW; it was Chevrolet—Cheve one foot and lay the other. But these cats didn't need to know that.

I smiled at Steadwell and said, "Check you later, man." I nodded over in Zeke's direction. "Let me go say hi to my neighbor." I plastered a smile on my face as I strolled across to Zeke, plopped into a seat, and leaned, friendly-like, across the table.

Zeke's face didn't crack. He crossed his hands in front of him on the table and just looked at me.

"I got a red bag at home that belongs to you," I said. Sullen eyes stared back at me. No response.

"I got your number, Zeke. What I want to know is, why? What'd I do to you?"

Zeke took a slug of his beer. "Don't know what you're talking about."

"Yeah? And eggs ain't poultry. I hear you like to draw on trees, too."

"Who told you that?"

"A bird. Cut the crap, Zeke. You've been giving me trouble from the beginning, and it's stopping now, hear me? And if your rent ain't paid by the first of the month, this landlord is serving your ass a notice to vacate. You got that? You don't know who you're messing with."

Fire sizzled behind Zeke's eyes, and he sneered. "You have no idea who *you're* messing with. I have papers Montcrieff gave me. You don't have the right to put me out, *nigger* landlord."

I stifled the urge to dust Zeke right then and there. The man had gotten on my last nerve. "Nigger is as nigger does, so who's the nigger now? Huh?"

I leaned closer and dared him to say another word, when, swear to God, Zeke's head snapped back, his eyes rolled around in his head, and his pupils changed colors—from deep brown to slate gray.

I ain't stupid. I recoiled and hissed, "You better cut that voodoo shit out. I mean it, Zeke." I took a quick look around the room. No one was watching.

In a flash, Zeke's eyes reverted to normal. He picked up his beer, casually, his voice even and untroubled. "Tree by a river, roots deep, cannot be moved," he said. Then he tipped the bottle and chugged.

I narrowed my eyes and stood. What the hell was Zeke talking about? The man was nuts. Too crazy to argue with, that's for sure. And arrogant—I think that's what bothered me the most. "Put paying your rent on your list of things to do, Zeke—before the first." I left him staring into space and went to take care of the business that I had originally come for, my appointment with Harry.

I made my way down a dim hallway to a back room and knocked on Harry's door. The door was answered by two of Harry's men—Blood Clots, members of his muscle brigade, Trinidadians, and relatives of Harry. Their size effectively blocked my view. One was bulked-up and the other was plain fat. See, if anybody got out of line with Harry, Fatty sat on you, while Bulk pounded your brains out.

The Black Sea parted, and Harry greeted me like his long-lost friend (which clued me I'd better be careful). But the Clots stood ready, waiting for me to breathe wrong, or give Harry some lip.

"Amos, good to see you," Harry said. I nodded at him. "We was just talking about you. How you and me niece doin'?"

By "We" Harry meant the criminal sitting next to him, Chazz Almendo, a Puerto-Rican brother who worked as a prison guard at Riker's and dealt mucho dope in and out of that facility.

"Hope you're saying good things, Harry." I looked him in the eye and told a bold-faced lie. "Catherine and me are doing okay. I like her. She's a nice woman." The last part wasn't a lie.

Harry waggled his finger at me and smiled. "Make sure you remember that."

In a millisecond, I flashed on what might happen if Catherine and me did get together. Breaking up, as the song says, might be hard to do. Jesus.

I returned Harry's smile with a weak-assed one, pulled the roll of money from my pocket, and placed it on Harry's desk. "That's all of it, Harry, with interest."

"Ah, Amos, good to know, you ain't forgettin' the vig." He accepted the money without counting it and scooped it into his desk drawer. "A man of honor, eh, Amos? Exactly why me thinking about doing business wit' you. Eh? You ain't doin' the numbers no more?"

"Uh-uh. Pursuing a new line of work."

"I heard, I heard . . ." Harry pushed together the tips of his fingers and fish-eyed me. "So? You making the money you want?"

Time ticked by. "No. But I'm making the life I want."

Harry wheezed and let out a laugh. "But a man can always make a little more money, ain't that right, Amos?"

I didn't respond. I didn't know what Harry was getting at. Harry got up and came around his desk and stood eyeball to eyeball with me.

"Smart, Amos. You got out of the numbers at the right time. New Jersey mob gone make gambling in Atlantic City happen. Naturally, that's gone put a squeeze on all the number businesses, eh? Got a proposition for you. Thinking about making you one of me boys—handling drugs on the East Side. What you think? More money than you can shake a stick at."

I rocked back on my heels. Harry had thrown a one-two punch. How to tell Harry? I wasn't in to shaking sticks.

I coughed. "Appreciate it, Harry, but I got . . . uh, allergies. Can't be around heroin, cocaine, things like that—they make me sneeze. I'd blow all the profits."

I said this with a straight face, while Harry stood thoughtful for a minute and squinted beady eyes at me. The Blood Clots behind me shifted uneasily. *Oh, shit, here we go.*

Then, Harry laughed out loud, which of course permitted his

three stooges to laugh. And the fools did, loudly—and they had no idea what the hell they were laughing about.

"Amos, you funny, man. Okay, I gone let you slide this one time. Think about it, is all. Don't want Catherine to end up married to no poor man, you know."

"Easy, Harry, easy, you're moving way too fast. Me and Catherine are just, uh, dating, you know?"

Harry waggled his finger at me again and purred.

"No-o-o problem."

No doubt about it, time for me to split. I said rapid good-byes to Harry and his three stooges, and hustled my butt on out of there. Exiting through the pool hall, I saw Zeke, crouched over his table, hands locked in a prayer position. Four empty beer bottles were lined up in front of him. He slid his eyes over me. Damn fool, drinking up my rent money. I slammed on my hat, hauled ass out of there.

Chapter 14

I caught a bus to Jersey. The rain poured steadily. No more pit-pat, it was the real deal. The bus bumped along and blew smoke out of its ass at every stop. Not much conversation from the other passengers. Even the kids were quiet. When you labor hard for a living, you're not too chatty after work. I had a seat by the window and watched the scenery lurch by.

My riding companion snored softly in the seat next to me. A brother about my age, dressed in tan cords with a lunch pail on his lap. Wondered why he didn't have a ride. To me, a man without a ride was like a man without a dick. Certainly not in control of his destiny. Was he on his way to work or coming home? And then I stopped worrying about him and thought about myself.

I fidgeted in my seat. This bus was taking forever—Herman's Cadillac Sales was going to close up on me. I glanced at my watch, an Omega timepiece that had escaped Bunky the pawnbroker. Six-fifteen. Herman's closed at seven on Saturdays. I had another forty-five minutes.

In Newark, I transferred to another bus that took me right up to the entrance of Herman's lot. Good thing, too, because my heel was raw, and specks of dried blood dotted the ankle of my socks. This walking crap was for the birds.

Herman stood at the entrance of the dealership's office with a shit-eating grin on his face—waiting for me, I guess. He probably saw me get off the bus. It was five minutes to seven.

Herman's belly hung low over his belt, and he tugged at his tie as he waited for me to approach.

"Hey, Herman," I said. "What you got for me?"

He stuck out his hand and pumped mine and clapped me on the shoulder. "Have I got a deal for you . . ." he said.

He led me down a long row of cars that shone under bright lights, with spanking-new upholstery I could smell as I walked by—swear to God. The sight intoxicated me, even while I felt like an inmate doing the last mile. When we reached the used-car section of the lot, Herman stopped in front of a shitty green clunker with a dented right fender.

"Give it to you for five thousand."

I looked around. Didn't see Baby anywhere. She must have found a home.

I turned back to Herman. "This is Amos Brown you talking to. I know you got something better than this."

Herman colored and cleared his throat.

"Of course, of course. You and me, we go way back, don't we? Played any poker lately?"

Herman once sat in a game with me and some of the boys, the scaredest motherfucker I ever sat down to a table with—didn't do nothing but sweat and fold all night long, and he asked this same question every time I saw him. Today it irked the hell out of me, and I snapped at him.

"Cut the crap, Herman, and show me something we can get serious about. I ain't got a lot of time, and neither do you, if you know what I mean."

Herman turned white as a sheet—as if I were some big-time mafioso who was about to take him out. Herman never did know the real deal about who I was or what I did. His imagination worked overtime and painted a picture of me as some hood from Harlem. I can't say I disavowed him of that notion—for a practical reason. Herman gave me better deals because of it. And some white types like Herman love to get chummy-chummy with the "darker race," and if they're criminals, it's a bonus. They wet their pants.

Hence, the poker game. Herman had slobbered all over me the time I invited him. But when he came face-to-face with the amount of money lobbed around the table, the bastard lost heart. Greedy Herman didn't want to part with his money, and whimpered each time he lost. Huh. The first and the *last* time he played poker with me.

So now here we were. Herman trying to game me, but he really didn't have the nerve. We moved to a back row of cars. A black '71 Caddie with tail fins caught my eye.

"How much for this?" I said.

Herman coughed. He did that a lot, and we both knew he didn't have no cold.

"Seven thousand," he said.

"For Christ's sake, Herman, you got to be kidding. How many miles on it?"

"Uh, I'll have to check."

He opened the door and peered inside. The interior was dirty, and the seats weren't leather. Damn, and no tape deck. I sighed. Beggars can't be choosers.

"Twenty-eight thousand miles. Runs good. This baby hums."

"Right, Herman. Tell it to your other saps. I'll give you fifteen hundred total."

Herman blanched. "Aw, Amos, you're the one who's kidding, right? I can't let this go for that kind of money."

"That's what I got, Herman, and I want to drive this car off the lot tonight."

"Well, uh . . ."

Herman hemmed and hawed—his way to avoid.

He said, "You really got no more money, Amos?"

I shook my head.

"Well, gee, Amos . . . okay. What say you give me the fifteen, and I'll put another fifteen under contract?"

"You mean I'm going to owe you?"

"Well . . . uh, yeah, Amos. You'll owe me. Spread it over a year."

I glared at him. He belched and stuttered, "T-two years if you like," he said.

It was hard to do, but I said, "One's year's long enough."

Herman beamed. "Well, all right then, good deal. I'll draw up the agreement right away."

He waddled off to get the papers and the keys. I walked around the car, inspected the tires, and shook my head one last time. The path of the righteous is one hell of a big comedown.

Chapter 15

Sunday morning, the pious and the good-timers passed by me on their way to church, as I scoured the interior of the clunker I had driven off of Herman's lot yesterday. This wasn't *Baby*, not by a long shot—naming this one *Stepchild.* I poured a mixture of water and ammonia on a sponge and purged the funny-looking spots that dotted the backseat of the car. I didn't care to speculate about the spots.

The car was ten years old, and the best Herman could come up with. I had to make do until times got better. Pissed me off that I owed Herman money. But it officially made me a member of the middle class.

I wrung out a sponge and caught the eye of an old woman with a pleasant smile who strolled by, Bible pressed against her bosom and carrying a large purse that could hold a week's worth of groceries.

I shouted to her, "Got a car note, ain't that something?" The church lady was dressed in white, a purple sash strung from shoulder to waist, and a starched hankie standing stiff in her dress pocket. A model of Christian charity, she lifted the edges of her mouth up in an uncertain smile and blessed me anyway.

I stood back and surveyed my work. Not too bad. I frowned. No tape deck. That was a drag. The interior had a few rips and tears, but Herman promised me the engine was solid. I sighed. As if I could trust Herman and his word. That white boy lied so much, he confused himself. But as much business as I had given the man, and as much business as I had sent the man, I expected him to do right by me.

I flicked a rag over a speck of lint left on Stepchild's exterior, ditched the water in my cleaning bucket at the curb, picked up my supplies, and went whistling into the house.

I had time to kill before my date with Catherine, so I deposited the cleaning stuff in the office and I started sifting through things in my father's crusty file cabinet. I had been putting this job off for a while, but today I felt energetic, so I got to work. I pulled a stool close to the cabinet and pulled out a drawer.

Jesus. I looked inside at all the junk, got discouraged, and slammed it shut again. Maybe I didn't feel like doing this after all. I tried the bottom drawer next. It had rusted shut, and I tugged until I jerked it open.

What was in it surprised me—an array of photographs, and on top, in the back of the drawer, I found an ancient Brownie camera protected by its own black leather carrying case. What do you know? My father had a hobby. Something inside me stirred. Would there be pictures of me in this pile? Growing up, I never remembered anyone taking a picture of me. I wasn't crying about it—it was just a fact.

Stone-faced, I picked up the camera and studied it. I looked through the viewfinder. Wondered how old something had to be before it'd be considered an antique. I put it aside, intending to hold on to it.

I surveyed the drawer crammed with pictures. The story of my father's life? Maybe. Was I interested? Not really. I'd gone this long without knowing anything about him. I was about to dump the pictures in a heap to make a Go pile when I stopped.

I had never seen a picture of my mother either. Aunt Reba had never shown me any, though I had pestered her. She told me instead not to dwell on my mother's death. What a load of shit. Her response never made much sense to me—then or now.

The pictures in front of me made me curious though, and I shuffled through the pile and scanned each photograph I pulled from it with greedy eyes. Would I even recognize my mother if I saw her?

I made a game of it. One by one, I continued through the pile. Bunches of women. Collectibles. My old man a connoisseur. Saw Twenties women with bow-shaped lips, marcelled hair, all gussied up in lush furs, dresses, or bathing suits—but I didn't see the woman I thought could be my mother. Or any baby pictures of me. Was I secretly hoping?

Photos of my father, Montcrieff, alone and together with Zeke, posed, both of them sharp as tacks in their salad days. The same pencil-thin moustache lined Zeke's upper lip and made him recognizable immediately.

Zeke of yesteryear looked more filled out. The men looked like brothers, my father the shorter of the two. Was the old fool crazy back then?

Scrawled across the bottom of one picture, the two dressed in suits and fedoras on their heads, was Zeke's signature with the promise "Friends to the end." *Well, buddy,* I thought, *you lied on that score.*

Some grudge with Montcrieff obviously festered deep in Zeke's soul, and I supposed my presence had dredged it up again. Well, Zeke had to learn that I was not my father.

I tossed the picture. Rummaging deeper into the drawer, I rescued a gold-framed sepia photograph of an older woman with smooth brown features and hair piled high upon her head, dressed in clothes three generations removed. My grandmother? Great-grandmother?

I searched the face for a resemblance to me—compared eyes, nose, hair. The old woman gazed mutely back. She wasn't giving up a clue.

While I stared, I felt a sting in my nostrils, and something unraveled inside me. Lost in thought, I was horrified when I saw that dots of moisture had collected upon the glass covering the woman's picture. I swiped at my face and at the picture with my undershirt, and wondered, what the hell? I was out of control here.

A lump rested in my throat. I shook myself like a dog shakes water. I bounced to my feet, dumped all the photos in the drawer. Then I hesitated and picked up the woman's picture again and moved the frame to my desk and stood it in the center. When the phone jangled, I jumped back, startled. Shit.

I lunged for the phone.

"Catherine," I shouted.

"Yes. Where *are* you, Amos?"

"Here. That's why I'm answering the phone, but I'll be there in fifteen minutes. Okay? Fifteen minutes."

Silence, then, "Amos, it's three-thirty. You were supposed to pick me up at three. Is this going to be your modus operandi?"

Dig this chick throwing Latin at me. What's she think, I'm dumb? She couldn't know, but Latin was one of my best subjects in prison-school. Aloud I said, "I apologize. On my way. Uh, stay sweet."

Blam. I hung up the phone and raced into my apartment. Took a one-minute shower, ix-nayed shaving, threw on some clothes, and flew out of the apartment. Two seconds later I flew back in to pick up my keys. For once I knew where to find them and I rejoiced.

Stepchild moaned a little as I threw her into gear, and I roared away from the curb as if demons were after me. I recalled the photographs. Maybe they were.

Chapter 16

I pulled up in front of Catherine's doorstep, checked my watch. Okay, it took me more than fifteen minutes. So another five couldn't kill, or could it? As I bounded up the steps to her front door, Catherine anticipated me and whipped the door open, purse in hand, sweater draped over her arm.

The daggers she shot pierced me to my core. In fact, I clutched my chest and fell back a step, as I attempted to explain.

You think it mattered? She ignored me big time.

"We have twenty-five minutes to make it to the four-fifteen show. It's at the Academy in Queens. Can we make it?"

She swept down the steps and waited by the car, arms folded. Then she did a double-take at Stepchild and looked up to me, the unasked question dancing in her eyes.

I leaped after her to do the gentlemanly thing and moved to open the car door for her. Wouldn't you know—the damn thing stuck. I pulled again. The car door wouldn't budge. "Don't do this to me, Stepchild," I muttered. I kicked at the door, and then I rattled and shook its handle.

While I kicked like a madman, Catherine strolled around to the driver's side, slid across the front seat, and opened the door.

"Get in, Amos, and let's go."

Still fuming, I hiked up my pants, swaggered around to the driver's side, and hopped in.

"That was a test. I wanted to see if you would pass it." I looked at her. "You did." I gunned the motor.

Catherine rolled her eyes at me, Stepchild hiccupped, and off we went to Queens.

The movie was good. At least we shared the same taste in entertainment. Afterward I took her to a homey Italian café I knew of that served great food. Eddie, the owner, always gave me top-drawer service. The food and wine made Catherine mellow, and put me in a better mood too. I glanced at her breasts a lot.

She sipped her wine and asked me, "So when are you going to tell me about your car?"

I hesitated. "Uh . . . now. My . . . my other car is in the shop."

"Really . . . ?"

"Cancel that. I sold the damn thing and paid off my debt to your uncle."

She set her glass down. I guess she saw I was having a hard time. "I'm sorry, Amos. I know you loved that car."

"Yeah, well . . ."

"Sometimes the Great Arranger conveniently moves things out of our lives when we get too attached to them—gives us a wake-up call. Lets us understand what's really important."

"The Great Arranger, huh? Is that the deal? Hey, listen, I know what's important. What's important starts with an M and ends with a Y." I couldn't help myself. I was agitated, and she was talking about some fucking Arranger.

"Money isn't the end-all and be-all for everything, you know."

"No? It sure as hell is, and if you don't think so, you're living in a dreamworld."

"What are you so upset about? Love's important. Family's important. Money is the least important."

When she mentioned family I looked up from my food and glared at her. Damn. There it was again. A bubble of emotion threatened to spill over.

I responded too loudly, "Don't want to bust your bubble, but love can be bought. On the corner of Fifth Avenue and 132nd

Street, for instance, you can get all the love you want for two dollars a pop. And family? I'm doing A-okay without one. It's highly overrated." The woman with the piled-on hair made a face at me from the recesses of my mind. I pushed the image aside.

"That's not love, and you know it. Amos, how can you put down something you've never had? You have no idea whether family is important or not."

I twirled my spaghetti, paused, and looked up at her. "You're right." I pushed a forkful of pasta into my mouth.

"That's it? No more argument?"

I sighed. "What's the problem now? I said you were right."

"But you don't really think I'm right."

She began to sound like Gloria, my ex. Why did women do this? I belched. Using my napkin, I wiped marinara sauce from my upper lip and deflected what I thought was turning into an argument. "I think you're cute."

"*Amos*."

"Look, in my book, money is important. And yes, I'm upset because at the moment I don't have any. Money equals status. Money equals respect. Money equals education. Money equals—hey, how about that? Tell me, what are you going to college for? And don't say to improve your mind, because I ain't buying it. You want to get yourself as far away as you can from a ghetto that represents L.O.M."

"What's LOM?"

"Lack of money, honey." Catherine sucked her teeth at me and stuck her nose way up in the air, away from me. I finished off my spaghetti and tossed down some wine and let the silence thunder.

In the stillness I counted the waiter's steps as he walked back and forth across the tiled floors. After a respectable amount of time elapsed I said, "Guess this means you're mad at me."

She balled her napkin up and flung it on the table. "On the money, *honey*."

What could I say? I looked at her breasts some more. She twisted her napkin around her finger.

Catherine broke the silence. I knew she would. "Amos, are you upset about your car?"

"Not my car. My life."

"It could be worse, Amos. Your life could be my life. How would you like to work forty hours a week, go to school full-time, and take care of a sick mother? With no social life."

I looked at her. For the first time we connected. We both smiled, and I reached across and took her hand. "You are cute, you know."

"So are you." She gritted her teeth. "And damn you, Amos, I put three kinds of lotion on my hands; don't you *dare* say anything about them."

My eyes widened in astonished protest. I didn't say a mumbling word. Besides, her hands were beginning to feel good to me. I paid the check and we left, arms locked around each other.

We got better acquainted on the way home. Stepchild's engine cut out on me three times before we reached Catherine's door, but all in all, it didn't matter.

Chapter 17

I sat on the front stoop and thumbed through the weekly edition of the *Amsterdam News*, Harlem's oldest newspaper, with my morning cup of coffee secure on the step beside me. The coming bicentennial activities filled the page. For the most part I ignored Gloria, who sat posed like a beauty queen on the stoop across the street, crossing and uncrossing her legs.

Since Catherine had just called me not ten minutes ago on her break at the hospital, I was pretty secure in the knowledge that Gloria and her nonsense had no power over me. The sun melted into my bones. I felt fine.

Things had settled into a routine in the landlord business. I had gotten used to imminent disaster, disaster, and holy shit. It occurred on a daily basis. Like day following night, I accepted the inevitability of it all. Like the alkies' credo, I worked on what I could change. The rest? Fuck it. That included Zeke, whose face I hadn't seen since last Thursday at Harry's. He slipped in and out of the brownstone like a night crawler.

Luigi inside was refitting the sprinkler heads. More shit on my credit card. HPD demanded I finish the work, and the court backed the agency up. Life gives you choices. HPD doesn't. I tried to hire black because black people needed the business, but black-owned businesses were scarce. The ones that existed often lacked either the people or the equipment to do a job right—and who wanted a job done wrong? Sick as I was of calling the downtown boys, I had no choice.

I sighed. Twenty years ago I used to be real critical of Adam Clayton Powell Jr. and those political types. Now I saw up close what they had been hollering about. I was the stupid one. In Harlem and all over the country an economic squeeze play was going on.

Government-sponsored programs filtered money into the wrong hands. Kickback, payback, double cross, double deal, and double dip was the way it went in Harlem. I sipped at my coffee as I considered the dregs.

I'd put myself in debt again to get the work on the brownstones done, and now I wasn't sure whom I'd rather deal with—somebody like Harry the Monkey Chaser or some of these piranhas that devoured black businessmen like so many small fish. No choice, I bent over and took it, right in the ass. I needed to hang tough, and there seemed to be a conspiracy out there that didn't want that to happen.

I fantasized about getting into one more poker game, make one more big play to get this load off of me, and looked upward for an answer.

Above me, the sky was spring-blue, the clouds a puffy white. Birds chattered and I heard the drone of traffic along Lenox Avenue. What I didn't hear was an answer to my new problems.

And then a sedan pulled up, and Detectives Bundt and Caporelli got out. Something about the way they walked toward me made me uneasy. Caporelli swaggered too much, and both of them had a hard time looking directly at me.

"Morning, gentlemen. You know you all left me with a big damn-ass hole. What can I do for you?"

Bundt spoke. "Got some news about that skeleton. Thought you needed to know."

Needed? What I needed was m-o-n-e-y. I didn't give food or a fuck about some bones in a wall. But I waited for him to continue.

"FBI forensics identified the skeletal remains—female, black, approximately twenty years of age. Figured she was cemented in the wall of your property thirty-five to forty years ago."

"Is that right?" I waited. "Good to know I'm not a suspect."

I smiled at the two of them. They didn't respond. "Something else?" I said.

Caporelli blurted, "It's your mother's skeleton." Bundt nudged Caporelli with his elbow.

I stared at the two of them. My heart stopped, but other than that I was cool. I took a sip of coffee and replied, "That's impossible. My mother died giving birth to me."

Caporelli said, "Yeah? That's what they told you? That's not what her sister says—"

Bundt interrupted. "Reba McKinley filed a missing person's report on her sister in 1945. We located Reba McKinley in Brooklyn and asked her to take a look at this." He offered me a photograph. I looked at it.

"Your mother's face left a perfect impression in the cement. Some items of jewelry were also identified by your aunt. A locket she wore. Sorry to break it to you, Mr. Brown, but it's your mother all right."

You know, I really liked the way he called me mister. I replaced the cup on the stoop and reached for the photograph. Without warning, something deep inside me cracked and split into ragged blocks of ice. An ice floe rafted through my veins and chilled me. I pressed my hands against my stomach to still the shaking. Through a roar in my head Caporelli talked, but the sound came at me muffled and distant.

". . . waited seven years to file a report . . . strangled . . . neck broken. A pity your old man's deceased. Might have wanted to have a conversation with him."

At the mention of my father, I raised my head. Caporelli lacked subtlety. I caught his drift, and a muscle in my jaw twitched.

"Murder this old . . . it ain't going to be easy to put the pieces together. You have information—anything about your mother that might help us?"

I stared back at the ground. I could offer no help.

"No, I can't help you," I said.

"Anything," Caporelli continued. "Something you've heard, from your father, other relatives?"

"No, I can't help you," I repeated. Caporelli cast a sideways glance at me.

Bundt said, "Mr. Brown, we're going to try, but to be honest, it's unlikely we'll ever find her killer. If you can think of anything useful to our investigation, let us know." He handed me his card.

I didn't trust my voice, so I nodded at him. He nodded back and the cops left in their car.

A squirrel clambered up and onto the branches of the oak tree. Minutes passed. The coffee grew cold. I stared across the street at the brownstone where my mother was murdered. Aunt Reba had lied to me.

I was seven years old and wore long gray pants. I was in Mrs. Schwartz's class at school, and my aunt Reba came to school. Why did I think of that? Gloria stood. She must have thought I was staring at her. She made a move like she was coming over.

The phone rang inside my building, coming from my office. I left Gloria standing—scooped up the paper, the cup, and my emotions, and disappeared inside.

Chapter 18

The next day, me and the sun got up at the same time. Dawn fingered its way into my bedroom. I sat on the edge of my bed thumbing through the Brooklyn phone book, looking for Aunt Reba's number. No luck. Maybe she'd gotten married. Disgusted, I tossed the thick book on the floor; it landed with a thud.

Satchels hung beneath my eyes. I replayed the scene on the front stoop for the millionth time. The questions I wanted to ask Reba looped around my brain like a hula hoop.

Dew glistened on the open window and I looked at it, then back at my alarm clock. Five-thirty in the morning. A two-hundred-pound bird with bronchial pneumonia chirped nearby. I slammed the window shut, lay back on the bed, and held my head. A mammer-jammer of a headache throbbed behind my eyes.

It was all God's fault. God must be a woman, 'cause she was always fucking with me. That's what women did—they fucked with you. Gloria came to mind. I rambled out loud—lack of sleep and pain in my head does that to me. Catherine's image floated past, her eyes huge and accusing. My eyes popped open and I peered around the room. Nothing there to "smite" me. I smiled grimly. The Arranger must not be paying attention.

Thoughts of what happened to my Mother replaced thoughts of Catherine. What did it matter if my mother died in childbirth, or some fucker offed her? Dead was dead. And that was that. But there was more to it. I couldn't leave it at that—not until I knew for sure who had killed her.

Montcrieff? Was it Montcrieff? My father? Frustration and anger made me ram a fist into my bedroom wall. That was stupid. The only thing that did was make a hole. Today, I needed to take action. I needed to talk to Reba. Get Bundt to give me her address. He seemed to be an okay guy—maybe he'd do it.

I turned on my side, pulled a pillow over my head, and tried to shut out morning noises and that stupid bird. Somewhere outside a garbage truck belched. I rolled on my other side. I couldn't quash the turmoil roiling inside, so for hours I watched daybreak turn to morning, and around eight o'clock I pushed myself up and got out of bed.

Both body and mind fatigued, I stood in the shower and let the water pour vigor and purpose into me. For twenty minutes I stood.

But after the shower all my movements seemed weighted and stuck in molasses. I toweled off, wrapping the towel around my waist, and shuffled into the kitchen. I brewed a pot of coffee, extra strong, and waited for it to perk. I looked up at the kitchen clock. Nine. Time to call Bundt.

I went to the bedroom, picked up my billfold on the nightstand with Bundt's card tucked inside, and dialed the Twenty-eighth Precinct. I was surprised when Bundt himself answered the phone.

"Detective Bundt here."

"Bundt? This is Amos Brown. Skeleton-in-the-wall Brown?"

"You don't need the description. I know who you are."

"Right. I need a favor. I want to find my aunt Reba. I'd like to talk to her about, you know . . ."

"You don't have her address?"

"Nuh-uh. We . . . we lost touch." There was a slight pause before Bundt answered.

"Really not supposed to do this but . . . tell you what, I'll give you the phone number. Let her decide if she wants to see you."

"Appreciate it."

"Hold on."

I heard the clunk of the phone as it hit the desk. I waited a minute, then he came back on the line.

"It's 5520 Nostrand Avenue." He immediately moaned and said,

"Aw, shit, I wasn't supposed to do that. I was supposed to give you the phone number . . ."

"It's forgotten already, Bundt. What did you say the phone number was?" He gave it to me, and I wrote the phone number down next to the address.

"Thanks, Bundt. I owe you."

He grumbled something unintelligible and broke the connection. I threw on some clothes and was out the door on my way to Brooklyn.

Chapter 19

Pots of roses, rhododendrons, and marigolds filled every cranny on the front porch of the small, trim Brooklyn house. Flowers nudged their blossoms against my pants and let me know I was an unwelcome intruder. I took in the place. Didn't add up—flowers and Reba?

I navigated my size-twelves through the minefield of pots and checked the number of the door against the address I held in my hand. Same number all right.

An old woman with runny-maple-syrup skin and bird eyes stuck her head through the curtains of the window on my left and stared out at me. I returned her stare and jammed the door buzzer hard.

Her head disappeared from the window. Seconds later I heard the click-click-click of locks being released and the door swung open.

"Stop ringing that bell, don't you see me coming? Amos? Is that you? Lord today. Amos Brown. Figured it wouldn't be too long before you'd come calling. Police already been here. Wipe your feet and come on in."

Out of habit, I did as I was told and entered the cramped vestibule. The woman who stood before me wasn't the Reba I remembered. This Reba had lost inches, and the years hadn't been kind. Wrinkles, like tributaries of some ancient river, crisscrossed the map of her face. The rod I had imagined as a kid to be soldered to her spine and inserted up her butt-hole had disappeared, leaving this new Reba bent over and frail looking.

I asked her straight out, "Why did you lie to me about my mother?"

She bristled and sparks shot from her eyes. "You come in here and accuse me, you might as well turn around and carry your black butt on out of here. I ain't taking your sass."

I clenched my jaw and said, "Listen, old woman, this ain't about you. I'm here to find out the truth about my mother."

"The truth?" she repeated. She turned and shuffled to the living room in her run-over slippers, and unfolded herself into a waiting easy chair. I assumed I was supposed to follow her, so I did. She pressed her hands together on her lap, her eyes riveted to mine with her birdlike stare. I took a seat opposite her on a stiff plastic-covered settee. The plastic snapped, crackled, and grabbed at my behind, and didn't want to let go.

Reba sniffed as if she smelled dog shit, then wrapped arms around herself and waited for me to speak.

"Well?" I said.

No response. And then I gave it to her. Words spewed from me like projectile vomit; I couldn't have stopped myself if I tried. "All those years ago—you lied to me. Did you know I grew up, old woman, thinking my mother's death was somehow *my* fault?"

Reba blinked and snorted. "Hmph. What you thought ain't had nothing to do with me."

My jaw dropped. Belligerent, she thrust hers forward. "Listen, boy, before you get on your high horse, you better remember who took you in when nobody else would. Who sacrificed precious years for your little hoodlum ass. What did I get for it, huh? Tell me that."

Unbelievable.

"She died giving birth to me—that's what you told me." I looked at her. It was useless. She'd never understand what she did to me. I shook my head. "Let's close the book on that, Reba," I said. "The deal is, somebody killed my mother. I want to know—did my father do it?"

"You not the only one hurting. My sister never deserved to be buried in no basement. She was too good for that."

"Well, that's what someone did. Did my father do it?"

Reba touched her throat where her next words caught. "How am I supposed to know?"

"Didn't I always hear you say how your sister was your best friend?"

"She was."

"Well? How were things between Montcrieff and Elizabeth? You had to know."

Like an inner tube deflating, Reba turned and blew a sigh into the room. "Why you want to know about Montcrieff? He's dead and this won't bring her back. Nothing on God's earth can bring her back." Tears started down her face.

"I've lived with that. But if Montcrieff didn't do it, I want to find the son of a bitch who did. Was Montcrieff violent?" I waited.

"Are you?" she countered. And then Reba fixed her eyes on a spot above my head—her next words difficult to hear. "I heard, the week before she left . . . before she disappeared . . . they took Montcrieff off to jail—the police released him two days later."

The fucking bastard. My hands turned February cold and it was June. I asked, "Why did you wait so long to report her missing?"

Reba hesitated. "I never thought . . . Not my duty. She had a husband . . . But when years went by, and no one heard from her, that's when I went to the police."

"And?"

"Said they'd look into it. Well, they didn't look too hard. Wasn't good relations between black folk and the police. I couldn't get in my head why Elizabeth would of run off and not tell a living soul. Where would she go? Our parents had died. We'd lived in Harlem all our lives. Where could a young girl go?"

I could tell it was a question Reba had asked herself before. I couldn't fill in any blanks. "Was there another man?"

Reba shrugged. "Maybe Montcrieff thought so." She snuck a glance. "You're tall, like your father."

I shifted in my seat. The plastic crackled. "Yeah, so I've been told." I leaned to the side, pulled plastic out of my behind, and got up, ready to leave. Something I had to do first. Tough to ask this witch for anything, but I did it anyway. I asked her if she had a picture she could part with.

She was surprised. "Of you?"

"No. *My* mother."

Her eyes bored into mine. I understood when she made the decision. She unfurled herself from her chair and crossed to an antique sideboard, its wood polished and rich. She opened sideboard doors and pulled out an inlaid wooden box, tucked away on a shelf. I moved to help her lift it. Together we placed it on top of the sideboard.

She tilted the lid back and carefully selected two pictures. One was a picture of two Harlem girls, Reba and Elizabeth, elementary school age, with hair plaited and dressed in pinafores, posed on the front stoop of a brownstone, the house on 131st—I recognized it as the one I also grew up in. The other was a sepia-toned wedding picture of a bride dressed in white lace.

Reba pushed the wedding picture at me. "Here, take this one," she said. She ran her fingers across the picture of the two sisters and returned it to the box. Pain crossed her face, and she grasped the box tightly. When I asked if she was all right she swatted me away. Then I asked a tougher question. I asked her if there were any pictures of me. She looked startled for a second, and then she shook her head. "No," she said.

The simple "no" told me what I wanted to know. I picked up my hat and headed for the door. "Thanks. I'll let myself out."

As the door closed behind me I heard, "Amos, next time call first, and I'll have some food ready for you."

I froze on the porch in disbelief, my hand still on the doorknob. She called me Amos. Reba had never called me Amos in all the years I'd been with her. Little Nigger, she'd always called me—and for the first five years of my life I thought that was my name.

A breeze eddied around my legs and whispered secrets to the flowers pressed against me. Did the blossoms look up and wink? Son of a bitch.

Chapter 20

Wet hung in the air. I flicked the sweat off my forehead that threatened to trickle into my eyes. I was hungrier than a *big* dog. Back in Harlem, I stopped to pick up a fried fish sandwich at Pan-Pan's on Lenox Avenue and wolfed it down in the car, hot sauce dripping onto my shirt, and then I cruised the hood, the streets thick with people. I nodded to some of the number runners working the streets, who returned a high sign as I passed.

All ages, colors, sizes, and shapes clustered on street corners, outside barber shops, beauty salons, grocery stores—catching up on gossip, telling lies, or signifying. American born or immigrant, didn't matter—all melded into the pastiche that was Harlem.

Reba hadn't given up much information, but what she said convinced me I didn't have to do much looking for the man that murdered my mother. He was as close as my skin. His ghost moved with me—was with me now. Seeing Reba revived a past I had shunted away.

Without much thought I made a spontaneous left turn at the next corner and found myself on 131st Street—the old neighborhood. I inched down the street until I came to a boarded-up and empty house—the house where Reba raised me. Signs of the Jolly Stompers, a Harlem gang, were evident. Spray paint had been graffitied across the front of the crumbling edifice.

Memories returned. I heard the shouts of long-forgotten friends urging me to come out to play. Jo-Jo, dead at fourteen, Rocky killed when I was in the joint. Bubba . . .

On the stoop, a couple of teenagers loafed and smoked reefer. I eased into an empty spot and parked the car. The teenagers paid me no mind. I looked at the building for a minute, and then noticed the stain on my shirt—the color of blood. Shit. I couldn't leave it. What was the matter with me? That spot, like the windowpanes in my office, disturbed me. All out of proportion to what it was, I know, but I couldn't leave it. I knocked about in the glove compartment and retrieved a paper napkin. I used spit to lift the spot, but it only made it worse. Damn.

A thump on my window and I shot clean up and off the seat, and hit my crazy bone on the door handle. Jesus. Ham Hocks stood there outside my car, grinning like a fool and waving at me. I rolled down the window, ready to cuss her ass out.

Instead she blasted, "Hey, Nigger Landlord, what you be doing over here?"

Like we were old friends or something. I ignored the disrespect and said, "You know this neighborhood?"

"Man, what you want to know? I knows everything."

"Is that right? If you know so much, how come you can't remember my name?"

"I knows your name all right. I just be funning with you, that's all. You Amos Brown. Your daddy Montcrieff Brown. Your mama dead."

I stared at her. Who was this woman? How did she know my daddy? I looked her up and down. She was one of those people you couldn't tell their age by their looks, who looked the same at thirty as they did at sixty.

I looked her over again. Jesus. A thunderbolt had hit her head—her hair stuck straight out all over. Her dress was grimy. She had few teeth left in her head. Whether they had been knocked out or had fallen out, who knew?

"How you know about my mama?" I said.

"Aw, man, everybody know about your mama. Leastways, now they do. But I knew your mama *when*."

The gossip machine—it roared through Harlem like one of them combines and mangled truth in its teeth like so much straw. I chewed on what she told me, and raised my eyebrow. "Is that a fact?"

She lifted her brow back at me and cocked her head to one side. The question and its inevitable answer hung in the air between us.

I pulled a five out of my pocket. Hocks grabbed at it, but I pulled it out of reach. She laid her roly-poly palm across my open window and told me, "Your mama be friends with my sister Doris."

That sounded like a lie as fat as she was. "Your sister Doris, huh? Where can I find your sister Doris?" I regretted the question as soon as it rolled off my lips.

Let sleeping dogs sleep. The past was the past.

Hocks pointed in the direction of two converted brownstones that stood side by side a few doors down the street, with the signs above the doors, THE CHURCH OF THE EVERLASTING ARMS and THE MOUNT ZION TEMPLE OF GOD.

"Axe for Sister Cawley at the Temple of God. She a deaconess." I hesitated for a second, then handed over the five. She stuffed the money between her big bazookas, then rolled off in the direction of Sixth Avenue.

I sat another moment. Hocks was probably running a number on me, but I hoisted my body out of the car anyway and turned my feet toward the Mount Zion Temple of God. Okay. So what if she was? Nothing to lose but time, and a five-dollar bill.

Dust angels rose up to heaven as Doris Cawley attacked the nave and aisles of the Temple of God sanctuary with broom and dust rag. Sister Cawley was no slacker. She was pissed at the interruption, but she told me that, oh yes, indeed, she was acquainted with the McKinley sisters. Grew up with them. And oh yes, Lord, that was one wild child. She obviously regretted the last remark, because God-loving Christian that she was, she fluttered one hand in the air and tried to erase it.

I eased her embarrassment and told her it was okay—what she thought of my mother was none of my business.

She looked at me as if I had lost a quarter's worth of sense and said, "I liked your mother."

Now I was confused, but when I asked for an explanation she jabbered at me about how sisters certainly were a cross to bear, and she went on and on and *on* about hers. She blamed Hock's downfall on men and liquor. Her sister's name was Dorothea. Can you believe it? Hocks? A Dorothea?

Then Cawley's eyes brimmed over with tears and in a sudden move, she grabbed both my hands and dropped like a lead shot to the floor. Well, shit, when she went, I went too—the woman was no Tootsie Pop. Both of us landed on our knees. She commenced to pray long and loud for two sisters who were, in her words, "lost to the world."

Since it didn't make any sense to get on the bad side of God, I stayed down for a respectful amount of time, but wouldn't you know, Sister Cawley went into overdrive and shouts of Praise God, Hallelujah, and Lawd, Lawd, Lawd rang around the church walls. It didn't take no Western Union telegram for me to get the message. I knew it was getting dangerous, so I pried myself loose from Sister Ton of Fun and split, stepping fast.

At the door I turned to see her still on her knees, praying. I intoned in response to her pleas, "God bless us, everyone."

I read that somewhere.

A note hung from the door of my office as I entered my building. What now? I backed up a few steps and ripped the note from the door. Wilbur. Good news—he wrote that Josie was coming home and he and Patty were on their way to Harlem Hospital to pick her up.

Just time enough. I checked my watch against the time on the note, charged out of the brownstone, and rocketed off to the hospital. When I banged through the lobby entrance, the group had just exited the elevator.

Josie looked beat, poor kid, but giggles erupted from her heart-shaped face when she saw me, and I smiled back. A week ago Patty had informed me about Josie's diagnosis. It was serious, sickle-cell anemia—a disease that afflicted black people and you can bet on it being a life sentence. The kid was going to have it rough.

I reached forward to lighten their load, and grabbed flowers, a small suitcase, a teddy bear, and the doll I had given Josie.

The selling point for the doll was that it wet itself. Would you believe it? No sooner did I have it in my arms than the doll trickled water. I scooted backward, but it was too late—a stream of liquid trailed down my leg.

Well, good to see I got my money's worth. Oh yeah, and the thing giggled too. It was doing that now. Yeah, the doll, Josie, Patty, and Wilbur doubled over—a regular laugh-fest, at my expense. Tell you the truth, I laughed some too.

Then I knelt by Josie's wheelchair and told her I was glad she was coming home. She grabbed my finger, and I waggled her hand back and forth.

Outside, the four of us piled into Stepchild, and for a moment, my own pain took a back seat and I let joy ride up front with me. We headed in the direction of Herb's Sweet Shop on 135th Street. Ice cream cones all around.

Chapter 21

Patty and Josie settled in, and I left Wilbur banging pots in Patty's kitchen. Smells of meat sizzling with garlic and onions wound down the stairs behind me as I descended the steps. My stomach talked to me, but I chose not to answer. At the bottom step, the smell of frying fish tangoed up from the basement apartment and past my nose. I ignored the hunger pangs and entered the office.

Behind the tenants' closed doors the living went on. A television blared suddenly, then quieted. Restless, I paced the floor of my office. When the front door slammed and the staircase creaked, I knew Winnie was home. A tap-thump, tap-thump coming down the staircase meant Zeke was leaving. I met him in the hallway, anger in check.

"Two days until the first," I reminded him. "You working on the rent?"

Zeke waved his cane in front of my face. "Call yourself lucky if you're alive by the first."

He tried to pass me, but I blocked his way. "You don't get it. You ain't on my 1040, Zeke. Understand? You ain't my dependent. If you don't pay the rent, I'm gonna have to put your butt out. And I really don't want to have to do that. Where's those papers you've been talking about?"

Zeke shot me a look that would have melted steel. I stepped away from him, the heat of his hatred too hot to handle. "Montcrieff, him promise me—" he said.

"Look, man, if there was something between you and my old man, I ain't had nothing to do with it. Whatever's rubbing you the wrong way, you better get over it, that's all I got to say."

"What you do in this life to deserve this house, eh? What back you break? That's all you got to say? Out of my way." Zeke swatted his cane at me. I jumped back, and Zeke hotfooted it to the door. In two steps I caught up to him and held his arm. Zeke's body shook with emotion. "Your father—a viper," he said. His lips trembled, his eyes grew hard, and he snarled, "And you, you just like him. How you like that?"

That shocked me and I froze. To be compared to Montcrieff? I released my hold on the old man and stepped back. Something moved behind Zeke's eyes, then, in a flash, he was out the door. Zeke was one spooky dude.

Was he trying to say what I had thought all along? That Montcrieff was responsible for my mother's death? It was clear he hated Montcrieff. What was incredible was how much the man hated me. Was he expecting me to be the same poison as my father?

I entered the office and poured myself a drink. Maybe I was going at this the wrong way. Each encounter with Zeke rocked me off my socks—and fueled tough questions. I sat unmoving for a while, unable to come up with answers. For the good it did, I could have spent the time picking lint out of my navel.

Friends forever, hmph. When did their friendship disintegrate and why? I needed to ask Zeke straight out about my father—and my mother, too. Which reminded me . . . I pulled my mother's wedding photo from my shirt pocket and pushed aside Zeke's voodoo bag. Zeke's bag—the man never denied it was his. A perverseness stopped me from getting rid of it. For me it had become a symbol of that something you wrestle with every day, the part of you that's ready to take you down, destroy you. If you let it. . . .

I propped the wedding photo next to the one of the woman with the upswept hairdo. My mother reminded me of Patty. In fact, she and Patty bore an outward resemblance to each other—wisps of women with small faces and troubled eyes, my mother, Elizabeth, only a year older when she died than Patty was now. But Patty was a young eighteen. Looking now, I thought my mother appeared much older. It was in the eyes. My mother's eyes looked older in the picture—harder. A knot twisted inside me.

Old at nineteen. What made her that way? Well, the answer was clear. Somebody knocks on you long enough you begin to look old before your time—man or woman. Or was the look on her face the result of a life spent fast and loose? Huh. Patty and my mother had that same fragility.

Hell, a summer breeze could knock Patty on her ass and swoop her the hell away. One thing was for sure—being mother to a sick child guaranteed that Patty was going to grow up fast from here on out. Too bad it had to be that way. The girl was overwhelmed, I could tell.

I leaned forward and peered into my mother's eyes. Who murdered you? No answer. Unfaithful or not, what kind of sick wimp does it take to kill a small woman like that? Like a summons to the devil, Montcrieff's image flashed in front of me. Fire ignited behind my eyes, a match struck suddenly. And what kind of man was I, content to stay in the house owned by the animal that murdered my mother? Was that what Zeke saw when he looked at me? I was stuck for an answer.

And then I wondered, maybe for the tenth time in my life, how someone like me managed to make it this far. Some of my youthful escapades had been narrow misses. Why did my mother die young, and I hadn't? I had trouble with a God who let the young die. Josie . . . if she lived to be twenty, she'd be lucky. Sickle-cell anemia takes you out early. Wasn't fair—why an innocent like her and not a hardhead like me?

Hell, I knew why. Alive today by grit and meanness. Knocked down, I'd get right back up and mess with you. Getting back up—the key to life, and what I did best. And damn it, no voodoo was getting the best of me. I slammed my hand down on the desk, and the sting of it propelled me into action. I stood up. The vibrations in this room were getting to me. I needed to do something.

My mother's picture looked naked. Didn't seem right that the stranger's photo should have an ornate frame while Elizabeth Brown went without, so I charged over to the file cabinet and rooted around until I came up with a small frame that fit the picture perfectly.

I set the frame on the desk, and restless, walked over to the window blinds. Light, needed some more light in here. I tugged at the cord and the blinds clattered skyward. I looked out at the familiar view, the afternoon sun so bright it singed, and I shaded my eyes from the glare.

Dirt layered the windowpane and distorted the panorama. I made a pass with my sleeve over the dirt. When the grime didn't lift, I rubbed harder with the heel of my hand. The dirt on the window smudged my hand and turned it black. Well . . . blacker. In that moment, my life seemed to be all about dirt, and there it was, encrusted on my windowpane.

Angry, I went to the closet, lifted a small bucket from the shelf, filled it with water from the bathroom sink, slopped in some detergent, swished a cloth rag in the water, and scrubbed the window. When I was well into it I discovered belatedly, the windows looked worse instead of better. The filth had streaked, not disappeared. Disgusted, I threw the rag back in the bucket.

Ammonia . . . I needed ammonia. Huh. Didn't have any.

Behind me, the two women on the desk had watched the disaster unfold with disapproving eyes—I caught their stares when I turned back.

I scrounged around in the cabinet and found a bottle of vinegar, so I ditched the bucket of soap, refilled it with clear water, and added the vinegar. My head ached now, but I worked through the pain until the windows sparkled. A penance, I think, and part answer to Zeke's question, "What did I do in my life to deserve this?"

Afterward, I popped two aspirins. Without water, the pills went down hard. A bitter taste caught at the roof of my mouth and eased its way down my throat. I was okay with that. I savored the bitterness, but it wasn't enough punishment.

I crossed to the file cabinet and jerked open the bottom drawer. Pictures scattered everywhere. I dropped to my knees and rummaged through the chaos for a picture of Montcrieff. What I stumbled upon was a picture of him, Elizabeth, and Zeke. The trio beamed up at me, smiles wide. One day in their lives they all had been happy—at least it looked that way. I combed their faces, hoping for some revelation.

If my mama was a slut and my daddy a killer, what the hell did that make me? Nothing. Nothing and nobody.

Shit. What was going on? The headache kicked my ass, and I doubled over, pressing my fingers against my temples to keep my head from exploding. I staggered to my chair and stumbled against the desk. The movement sent the bag flying to the floor. I retrieved it, and head throbbing, I stuffed the spilled stones and feathers back into the bag.

Then I slumped into the chair and waited for the aspirin to do its stuff. To divert myself, I focused on the bag and passed it back and forth between my fingers. The Elmira chant—a mantra from my long-ago prison stretch—came to me, unbidden, from deep within, and ran laps around my head.

"I'm a person, not a number. I came from somebody, I'm not a nobody."

The irony choked me. Slivers of tears danced at the edge of my eyes. I wrapped myself up in a cocoon of silence—and I was back in the joint at Elmira, in solitary lockup.

Chicken wire angled down from the ceiling and kept me stooped over, unable to stand. Bread. Water. And a pot to piss in. My third day in a strip cell, dressed in socks and underwear. With my fingernails I could scrape filth off the walls, it was that thick. And the smell of urine burned my nostrils and made my eyes water.

The odors of a hundred men were locked into the fibers of a funky blanket wrapped around my body—my only protection against the dankness and slime of the cell. That's when the chant began, back in those days, those first days in solitary.

My heart tattooed rhythms against my chest, breath rasping like death inside my throat. Back then I clung to the words, tuned out everything else. The cries and moans of men in pain inside the prison walls, they faded into nothing. Quiet. Time stopped, days passed, and I survived.

Nothing and nobody could touch me. Not that time or the times after—they couldn't break me. And to think, I wasn't as old as Patty. My lids grew heavy and I dozed in my chair, the chant on my lips.

Spirits floated in the air around and through me. I shuddered at each pass through my body. Son of a bitch Montcrieff wanted to hurt me, but I ran a shiv up his gut. My mother, Elizabeth, young and desirable, body pulsing red-hot under a winking neon light, trolled for tricks as I watched, horrified. I reached out, tried to save her, but instead my arms wrapped around Deaconess Cawley. She and Big Butt hovered above me, suspended in the air by the flapping of their angel wings. Cawley screamed, and the sound pierced my soul. I let go, and she shot straight up to heaven.

Me and Dorothea—Big-Butt Hocks—settled on the ground amidst the dirt and filth. Hocks cackled and passed me a bottle of T-Bird. It went down my throat like Drano, and liquid fire exploded in my gut—turned to blood and gushed like a geyser out of my nose and mouth. I lay, unable to help myself, slowly bleeding to death . . . surrounded by stench and filth.

The ring of a doorbell jolted me and snapped me upright. I looked out the window at Catherine, toe tapping, standing on the doorstep.

The last person I wanted to see. I wiped the sweat from my face and waited—maybe she'd go away. When she didn't, and rang the bell again, I went to the front door, cracked it open, and stuck my head through.

"Yeah?" I said.

She responded with a questioning look and said, "It's been a while."

I didn't offer up an apology. What would be the point? I lamely shrugged my shoulders and hoped that would suffice.

"I heard about your mother, Amos." She studied her feet for a moment, and then she looked back up at me. "From someone else."

She had on sandals and hot pink toenails peeked out of them. I couldn't look her in the face, so I too, looked at her feet. I didn't say anything. She gave me the once-over and said, "Let's take a walk, okay? To the duck pond?"

"Uh, no, thanks."

"C'mon, Amos . . . it'll do you good."

Her toes fascinated me. "Another time," I said.

So soft I almost didn't hear, she said, "Amos, if you hold your pain, it festers." When she got no response she touched my sleeve lightly, turned, and walked down the steps.

Electricity shot through my body at her touch. The effect made me wake up to what was happening, but I was a loner who needed to be alone. And though I felt guilt, I couldn't handle the moment and Catherine too.

I shouted after her, "I'll call you," which sounded like a lie, even to my ears.

She acted like she didn't hear me. She hailed a gypsy cab. It stopped. She got in and the cab drove away.

Sometimes I could smack myself. This was one of those times.

Chapter 22

In the amber light of early evening, I walked to the duck pond at the tip end of Central Park at 110th Street. The sultry heat of summer drew toxins from my body, and my headache diminished. Dripping with sweat, I entered the park.

At the entrance on 110th Street, junkies nodded and sat with backs braced against trees, their odor ripening in the heat of the sun. Other junkies sprawled comatose on the rich green of grass. In a game of catch, juvenile delinquents threw softballs across the inert forms, gang hats pulled low on their foreheads. In times past, this end of the park used to be a pleasant place to visit. Graffitti was everywhere. Obvious to me Catherine hadn't been here in a long while.

Banners hung slap-dash around the park, advertising the bicentennial activities. A parade of baby carriages rattled past. Young mothers guided buggies along the path encircling the pond, and steered their young ones past an obvious drunk, bottle in hand, who staggered in between them.

People strolled past in both directions. I joined the strollers, turned left, and headed for the boathouse. Seniors sat on benches, solo or in pairs, bodies hunched, expectantly waiting for a word, a look, or a smile—from anyone. Or waiting, maybe, for the sun to set, or death to come—whatever came first.

I nodded at one old geezer. He touched his cap with a "Hi, partner" and gifted me with a smile that lit up the park. My mood improved; my head no longer ached. Maybe the walk had done some good.

Past the boathouse on the east side of the pond, near Fifth Avenue, I chose a spot, climbed down some steps, and sat at the pond's edge. Trees hugged the pond's perimeter and lent some shade. I opened my shirt and wiped the sweat from my chest. Ebony children, roasted by the sun, carried the musk of hard play and summertime. Small bodies streaked past and squealed with delight.

I settled into place and sat for a long time. My eyes took in a mother duck and her brood trailing serenely over placid waters. Behind the pond, on the other side and rising from the ground, was the knoll I used to climb as a kid. Played cowboys and Indians on that hill—while Aunt Reba waited well past the dinner hour, strap in hand, for me to return home.

Did Montcrieff kill Elizabeth? I was certain he did. The ducks paddled their way across the pond. I followed their progress with my eyes. When you least expect it, the answer comes. A memo from nature—time to get my ducks in a row.

The sun stepped down from the last edge of sky, the streetlights blinked on, and I brushed twigs and leaves off me and stood.

Yeah, once again, I got back up, like I always did.

When I returned home it was a little after nine. I made a call, picked Catherine up from work, and drove her back to my place. We didn't talk much. That was good. I ditched the lights and we fell into bed, my hands gripped her ample ass, and all my problems melted away, along with planet Earth, the cosmos, and the entire universe.

Each thrust and groan rocketed me closer to heaven. Catherine's body arched beneath mine, her body convulsed, and she wrapped her legs tight around my waist. Sweet pain. I gasped, squeezed my eyes shut, and discovered the meaning of life—deep in Catherine's womb.

Bliss spread through my body, rippled past sinews, on down to my toes, and, like snow melting on a mountain, I eased off of Catherine and fell, exhausted, into a deep and heavy sleep.

Throughout the night, the caress of gentle hands played melodies against my body as I slept the sleep of the dead. Come daylight, Catherine was gone.

Chapter 23

The next evening I gazed at the red, amber, and purple colors that stretched across a Fourth of July sky and it was still June. Dusk gentled down in Harlem-town. Streetlights snapped on, and residents poured into the muggy night and parked their rumps on porches and stoops.

At the end of the block, men and women camped on folding chairs, kitchen chairs, and wooden crates, clustered close around a rickety card table set smack in the middle of the sidewalk. A naked lightbulb dangled overhead from a makeshift contraption erected solely for the card players' convenience. A bid whist game was in progress and it was intense. The slap of cards and protesting voices or hoots of laughter rang up and down the whole block.

Teenagers lolled against buildings and stoops. A miscreant child chased a ball into the street, and a she-wolf bellowed his name and threatened a blistering butt-whipping.

I held a cold bottle of beer next to my cheek for a long minute before I allowed its liquid foam to ease down my throat. Somebody had torn half of my FOR SALE sign off the oak tree in front that I had labored to put up this morning, and the FOR SALE sign I had put on the brownstone across the street had disappeared altogether. The rest of the day I had holed up with Tolstoy's *War and Peace*. Depressing as hell.

Gloria had kept her distance since moving in, thank God. The woman was working on getting hooked up fast, and so far as I could tell, she was having some success. Gloria on the prowl was a sight to behold. She had "dates" every night. Not hooking, just looking, she told me. I wished her luck in the worst way. Anything to take the heat off me.

With no food in my belly—the bologna sandwich didn't count—I was getting a tad light-headed. Oh well . . . I gulped another swig of beer. Brewskies—that's what white people called them, brewskies. What the hell, the "brewskies" dulled the pain and helped me chill. One by one I separated the events of the past two days, pigeonholed them, and took a deep think with each swallow.

I was finishing up my third brew when Miss Ellie came out of the brownstone across the street and waved. She wore a flowered print dress with spaghetti straps and yellow high-heeled shoes. From this distance and after three beers the old woman looked damned good. She fluffed her hair, set a cushion on the stoop, and held a paper bag high for me to see—I knew what it was—and called over to me.

"Hey you. Amos Brown. What you doing? Bring your fine brown self over here and keep an old lady company."

Looking at the loveliness of Miss Ellie I thought, okay, being seduced by a seventy-year-old woman wasn't the worst thing that could happen to me. Catherine crossed my mind, but I reasoned this didn't have nothing to do with her. It took all of maybe twenty seconds for me to join Miss Ellie on the stoop. She pulled a bottle out of the brown bag she held and poured Johnny Walker Red in generous amounts into two paper cups.

"Amos, a shame about your mother." She downed her drink in one gulp. I blinked at the disappearing act, mumbled a response, and followed suit. The drink worked its magic immediately—I don't know if it was the heat or what, but my whole body tilted suddenly to the right, and damned if I didn't hear a bell clang somewhere. A warning? Or was it the beers I'd consumed? The world shifted back to center, but for a minute I lost my balance and sat down hard on the stoop.

"Yes, that was one beautiful woman," Miss Ellie said.

"You knew my mother?"

"Of course I did. I was living here way before your father took over this building. She was—"

"I know . . . wild."

Miss Ellie drew back and looked at me as if I were crazy. "Who told you that?"

I tried to think. "Reba?"

Miss Ellie shook her curls and laughed, and without asking, poured us both another shot. "Well, I know Miss Reba, and all I can say is, consider the source. She's putting something on your mama that looks better on herself."

I didn't stop her from pouring, though I should have. "You're kidding. Tight-assed Reba?" I said.

"Honey, your aunt Reba's ass wasn't always tight, let me tell you."

I sipped the Johnnie Walker this time.

"Fact is, Miss Reba had her some men now. Plenty Negroes drooled over her. Thought she was God's gift to men. Plucked her feathers when . . . Oh, never mind."

Miss Ellie looked sideways at me and shook her head again. She said, "Yeah, I remember one time, Reba and me, honey, duked it out at Connie's Inn, over Sweet Dick Wilson—"

"You fought?"

"Yeah, baby—sorry, Amos—had to kick her ass over Sweet Dick Wilson, a drummer I used to go with. Don't let nobody tell you different, Miss Reba was a firecracker. Oh-me-oh-my, Sweet Dick—now that was a good man."

"So what happened to Sweet Dick?"

"What you think? The man was a bumblebee, always looking for a flower. Sucked it dry, then the bumblebee moved on. Left a sting in my tail, swear to Jesus. Umph, Sweet Dick was something else."

She hung in her reverie for a few minutes more while I entertained my own private thoughts, and then I asked her, "Miss Ellie, think Montcrieff killed my mother?"

"Lord, child, why you ask me something like that?"

"I know he beat her.""

"You do? How you know that? You were there?"

"I heard Montcrieff was carted off to jail a week before my mother showed up mis-s-sing." Uh-oh. I was losing it—better lighten up on this alcohol.

Miss Ellie thought a minute and said, "You talking about the time Montcrieff went ape-shit and threw a chair out the window? Yes, Lord, that was something else. Yeah, I remember him being arrested, but it wasn't for hurting nobody. It was for throwing furniture out the window."

"Why in the hell did he frow—*throw* furniture out the window?"

"I ain't a crystal ball, but the way I heard it, somebody had done something to Elizabeth and he was upset."

"He never hit her?"

"Well now, Amos, you backing me up in a corner. Ain't something I'd swear to, Montcrieff did have a temper and all, but I know he was head over heels in love with your mother."

"Yeah, but you and I both know, some people have a strange way of showing love."

Miss Ellie read the expression on my face, up-ended the last of her scotch, and disappeared into the house and returned with a full bottle of 151 rum and poured.

"Listen, Amos, all I know is, your father never hit me."

Puzzled, I looked at her. "Why would he hit you?"

Miss Ellie averted her eyes and adjusted her dress. "Well . . . Montcrieff needed a little comfort after your mother left—uh, that is . . . disappeared—and well . . ."

She didn't have to say any more. But I looked at Miss Ellie in a new way. She had been capable of whipping Reba's ass. Did she have a motive for murder? Was she capable of sealing a person into a wall—and into the same building she lived in?

A wave of horror came over me and I chased away the morbid and accusing thoughts with yet another slug of Miss Ellie's liquor. This damn alcohol was making me paranoid. I set my cup down.

Some neighbors joined us on the stoop and we passed the rest of the night in idle chitchat. Miss Ellie could handle her liquor and left me in the dust. The old lady didn't miss a beat, and kept up with the hardiest of the drinkers.

At one o'clock in the morning, six of us sat sprawled on the stoop, shooting the breeze and passing the bottle around. Miss Ellie waxed nostalgic and talked about Cotton Club days and the celebrities she knew. The Duke—Duke Ellington, that is—Lena Horne, Bricktop, the Astors, fighter Jack Johnson, and I don't know who all. Then she performed a tap number in front of the stoop, and I noticed with uneasy awareness the muscles in her legs and arms. All of us applauded. She was damn good. But I wondered.

When I saw Zeke come home, that put an end to the evening. I sprang to my feet, a top spun out of control, and fell over myself. Slurring good-bye to Miss Ellie and the others, I lurched with purpose across the street.

Not my business, but where the hell was Zeke coming from this time of night? The old man must be a bat—he kept bat hours. And he was old enough to be my father. What was with him? A girlfriend somewhere? I caught Zeke before he entered the building. I grabbed him by the shirt and slammed him against the front door so hard his false teeth rattled in his head.

"Pay me my rent, man. Don't make me box you up."

"You're drunk."

"If that's what it takes to collect from you." At that point I didn't give a rat's ass if what I said made sense or not. Zeke and his arrogant ass pissed me off. I focused real hard on his nose, and it helped steady me.

"Let's take this inside," Zeke said.

"No, outside, let's take it outside." I hung from his shirt like a clothespin turned upside down. The man was overdue for a knuckle sandwich and I sure felt like giving it to him.

People passing on the sidewalk gawked, and the bunch with Miss Ellie stood and stared at us. An embarrassment I couldn't seem to help. I let go of his shirt, swayed, and leaned sideways, my balance unsteady. Zeke caught me by my arm and half carried me inside.

"Tomorrow I'll bring you the papers," he said.

I said again, "About my rent, Zeke."

"I don't pay rent."

The conversation went round in a rhythmic circle, in time with the swirling ceiling and the undulating stairwell. It was too much. My eyes crossed.

" 'Zactly what I'm saying. That's why I got a problem with you, Zeke. You ain't paid rent since I've been here."

"Montcrieff made an agreement with me. I don't pay rent. I have the papers," he repeated.

What was it about Zeke that made me so angry? I pushed him up against the wall, jammed one arm against his chest, and leaned on him, hard. His eyes bucked.

"You lying sack of shit. Show me."

"In my room. I have to get them."

"Get 'em. I ain't going nowhere."

Zeke gasped for breath. I let up on him. He shook me off angrily and climbed the stairs to his apartment. I watched him go, saw the ceiling spin, and slid like sorghum molasses down the wall.

Chapter 24

Damn sun again. Somebody should shoot it. I inched my eyelids open, and the full force of daylight attacked. I wrenched the bedroom blinds shut and fell back on the bed.

Counting to ten, I lay there. It didn't help. Yesterday's clothes stuck to my body. I filled my lungs and counted to ten again. That same bird cheeped outside my window. My mouth tasted scummy, and I needed about a gallon of water to stem the awful thirst.

I rolled on my side, and a paper rustled underneath me. I counted to ten one more time, pushed myself to a sitting position, and uncrumpled the paper.

Through bleary eyes I saw that it was a copy of a signed and notarized document, Parts I and II. A serious bit of legalese. I read on. "For Services Rendered," it said, dated November 15, 1937. A long-ass time ago. At the bottom of the page, whatever had been Part II of the document was ripped from the page.

I tossed the paper on the floor and stood up. A mistake. The room spun, I let out a groan, and fell back on the bed.

Elbows on knees, hands steadying my head, I tried to stop the spinning and get my brain to work. Why the pussyfooting around—why didn't Zeke tell me about this straight off? Why keep avoiding me? Zeke was a strange bird, and one I wasn't about to take time to figure out—especially this morning with my A-1 hangover.

I rose slowly this time. "For Services Rendered." What could that mean? He and Montcrieff were ace-boon-coons. Did this agreement buy Zeke's silence? For what? Murder? Maybe. The agreement probably wasn't worth the paper it was written on. I retrieved the document from the floor. Better have an attorney check it out. Aw, shit, what the hell did I care?

I went to the kitchen and sucked on ice cubes, then stuck my head in the refrigerator and left it there for a few minutes. The weather was going to be a bitch today. It was ten o'clock and it was already hotter than hell. Somebody leaned on the front doorbell, but I didn't care. Didn't care at all. Wasn't going to answer it. Ever. Fuck 'em. Fuck 'em all.

I prowled around the apartment for the rest of the day. The doorbell rang constantly; I could hear the phone in the office ringing too, but I wasn't answering.

By evening-time I got antsy, and made a few phone calls to my boys—guys I had previously hung with. That old fever came back. I was looking for a game, and a way out.

Hooch Rawley, a friend and former inmate with me at West Coxsackie State Prison from years ago, turned me on to a high-roller's game on the third floor of the Cecil Hotel, a place that catered to the entertainment set and other fly types as well as the criminal element.

Money was the equalizer and social leveler. Five hundred would let me sit at the table. Whether I stayed depended on the run of the cards.

I dressed for the part—put on a lightweight grey suit that I hadn't sacrificed to Bunky's, an emerald tie and a light green shirt. Scrounged through my office and found five bills tucked away in a locked box, and put paper in my inside jacket pocket. *Cecil, I'm coming.*

Stepchild was parked at the end of the block today. My usual space in front of the brownstone had been taken by one of the congregants of the Assembly of God Christ Church located at the opposite end of the block. In fact, most of the parking spaces on the street were gone, and cars were double-parked. Summer was revival time at a lot of churches in Harlem, and the church on our block was whooping it up with plenty of *joyful noises* and jubilation that carried down the length of the block.

As I approached the corner where the church was, four junior hoodlums, all under age ten, pitched pennies against the building's wall, near where my car was parked. I asked, "You mind?" and took a coin from my pocket, put a little heat in the toss, and slammed it against the wall. It hit, held, slid, and puckered up and kissed the wall. I gathered up the pennies and told the little buggers that's what they get for gambling. Since I was bigger than them, they didn't attack—they settled for tight jaws all around.

Stepchild burped and hiccupped when I tried to start her. In spite of the kids' jeers, I got her going and took off for the Hotel Cecil, adrenaline pumping.

Most of the players at the Cecil I knew, so it was no problem to join the game. T-Bone Thompson, a blues singer who teetered for years on the brink of real success; two warped lawyers, one a prosecuting attorney; and Toothpick Flynn, who owned a bar on Lenox Avenue plus a numbers operation, made up the assembled group. Harry the Monkey Chaser was there too, sitting smug in his chinchilla hat. Nobody reminded Harry it was summertime.

The usual hangers-on hung around the room, swilling booze and watching the action. No smoking was allowed because of Harry's asthma, so nicotine fever had people coming and going, in and out of the room. Didn't bother me, I didn't smoke, but some of the players got real fidgety. Twelve hours in a box playing poker is not pleasant. If the smells don't get you, the smoke usually will. Thank God for Hotel Cecil's air-conditioning and Harry's no-smoke rule.

A slit with her lungs falling out of her dress served drinks, sandwiches, and complied with requests. Part of her job, I guess, was to bump titties against every man that sat at the table, and those that lined the room. Each bump yielded her a five-spot. If you groped her ass you had to give up a twenty. Anything else you took it outside. She stuffed the money between her titties and it looked to me like she was having a hell of a night.

Cards fell loose and fast. I hit on the first hand and bumped my stake to two grand. After that I grew reckless and didn't much care. The next five hours raced by. I was in my element. I fed my fever and let it burn white hot.

It burned all night. At two in the morning I began to lose. I was a thousand down when I, at last, pulled out my paper. Everyone around the table turned their faces to the off position and looked blankly at me. The bluesman spoke first.

"What the hell is that, man?"

"Deeds to two brownstones in Harlem."

Silence. One of the lawyers with messed-up teeth spoke next. "What do you think this is? Monopoly? Are we playing Monopoly here? You can't bet brownstones, Park Place, or the Reading Railroad. If you ain't got the money, you got to get up."

Toothpick chimed in, "Yeah, boy, what you think this is?"

I said in a reasonable tone, "Think about it. You could all use a tax write-off."

The whole table laughed as if what I said were the funniest thing going. Harry the Monkey Chaser cackled the loudest and said, "Who pays taxes? Huh? Anyone here?" The table roared again.

Then he turned serious and looked at his watch. "Got to take care of some business back at my office. Let's move the game over there. Amos, bring the deeds. I'll spot you for your brownstones."

He unfolded himself from his chair. "How much you think they're worth?"

I didn't blink. I said, "Fifty thousand each."

Harry laughed and moved a silver dollar through his fingers. "A joke, eh? Fifty thousand for *both*."

"Okay, forty thousand each." I called myself being firm.

Harry exploded. "You deef, man? What I want with your brownstones? Fifty-five thousand for both. Take it or leave it."

"I'll take it," I said, before Harry had a chance to change his mind. It was no problem for me to let Harry think he had gotten the best of me.

With Harry's offer, everyone knew the ante had rocketed. An electricity shot through the room, and people grabbed jackets, money, cocaine, and vacated—tootie sweetie, like the French say. The city attorney copped out, but the rest headed over to Harry's place.

Walking to my car, I knew I really didn't care which way the wind blew. After all, nothing from nothing left nothing. I gave it over to fate, put it in the driver's seat.

Stepchild must have been listening. When I tried to start her, she threw up on me.

Stuck. It was after two o'clock in the morning and no cabs in sight. Not even a jitney cab. Damn.

I kicked Stepchild's tires. No response. I left the car and footed it to Harry's place. Did I mention that Harry didn't like to be kept waiting? I hoped to God the car would be in one piece when I returned.

When I got to Harry's, all eyes were on me as I sat down to the table. Harry spoke. "Thought you changed your mind. Waiting on you. My deal. Five stud. Four up, one down. Cut the cards, Amos."

Chapter 25

The next four hours slid by like molasses in July. I was up and I was down. You'd think it would be easy to lose fifty-five gees, but I'm here to tell you, it wasn't. Four A.M. came, four of us remained at the table, all sweating in a second-floor room at Harry's, no air-conditioning. The air was close and steamy. No one complained. The game was so intense Harry finally took off his hat. We were back to playing five stud.

Toothpick Flynn was the big winner so far, the lawyer came in second, T-Bone had dropped out and was fast asleep on the couch, Harry remained about even. Me, I was down five gees, and it was my deal.

"Dealing the cards. Five, queen, nine, my ace. Your queen, Harry." I said, "Ace bets five hundred."

Toothpick scooped up the five-card, and turned it face down on the table. "Fold."

The lawyer sighed and said, "Play 'em like you got 'em. I fold."

Toothpick left the table to recharge his drink. Harry and me sat looking at each other. The lawyer just looked.

"Me and you, Harry. What do you say?"

"Call."

"Coming out. Possible jack queen. Uh-oh. Another queen. And a deuce. Pair of ladies bet, Harry."

Harry smiled a shit-eating grin. "Five thousand."

"No respect for my aces?" I said.

"Make me a believer, Amos."

"Going to do that." Harry's smirk was getting to me. "Here's your five and bump it another ten. Show my aces some respect, Harry."

The lawyer let out a groan.

"You're lying, Amos. Call."

I dealt two more cards. "Here we go. Queens with a . . . king, and—a pair of deuces with an ace kicker. On you, Harry."

"Me boy. It's gone cost you. What you got left, eh?" Harry calculated, and came up smiling. "Thirty more, let's get real."

T-Bone suddenly woke up and so did I. The moment had arrived. I maintained my composure on the outside, but my heart did a few skips. "Call."

I kept my eyes on Harry and dealt a jack to him and a seven to me.

Smooth as silk, Harry said, "Way I figure, you ain't got nothing else to bet."

T-Bone crept forward to the table and took a place behind the lawyer. The lawyer shot quick looks between Harry and me.

"I got ten more, Harry, ten more."

I didn't waver. A baptism. Washing myself clean. Brownstones disappearing in a cloud of smoke and a heigh-ho, Silver. I smiled at Harry. A river of sweat ran down my body. Turning a new page in the book of life. For a second I flashed on my tenants. Sweat trickled on my cards. I wiped them. Harry saw the gesture and considered what his next move would be. The man didn't like to lose, and he also wasn't about to punk out. Harry dripped a goodly amount of sweat as well.

"Okay," Harry said. "Ten. But why be chicken-shit about it, eh? Another ten."

I looked at Harry and reminded him.

"We set a limit, Harry. You going to live up to your word?"

Harry glanced around at the others in the room and smiled. "What's the matter, Amos? Got no balls?"

"No, Harry, I got no more money."

"A shame. You wouldn't have that problem if you worked for me."

"No, I'd have another problem." Harry waited for me to explain.

I said, "The risk."

He laughed. "Ain't no more risk than you taking here. Tell me true, ain't you gambling your life?"

That hit me where it hurt. I looked at the others. They knew something was going on besides cards. I snapped back, "What is it, Harry? Why you want Amos Brown in your pocket? Your pocket ain't fat enough? Drugs are evil, invented by the devil."

Harry's eyes closed to slits again, glowed like a fiend's; his wheeze menaced.

"What you saying, Amos? You think you better than me? Better than *me*? It ain't about evil or good. It's about money. Me chased the great American dream, and me caught it. You hear me? Me caught it and wrestled it to the ground. How else you think a black man's gonna make any real money? I'm talking Rockefeller real, Dupont real. Tell me that. I ain't never forced nobody to take drugs. Ever. I don't have to." The room was silent.

Harry was annoyed. I didn't back down, I moved on. I smiled, gave Harry a thumbs-up, and picked up the deck of cards. I dealt the last card. Down and dirty. "Call," I said.

Harry's sour face disappeared. He grinned like the cat who ate the cream.

"Put your money on out there, Harry."

"Put your marker up."

I complied and shoved the two deeds into the center of the table. And stared Harry down.

From nothing. To nothing. It all meant less than nothing to me.

Harry flipped over his card and slammed it down. An eight. No help, but he didn't need it. His queens would still beat a pair of deuces any day.

I was at the bottom of a vortex, traveling at the speed of light, yet things unfolded in front of me in the slowest of motion.

I turned my card over, and I gasped. So did everybody else. A deuce. I was stunned. Three deuces. Shit. Harry leaped out of his seat, upsetting cards and money.

"Game's over," Harry announced.

[illegible]

Lamb, [illegible]

He answered, "[illegible] ask [illegible] of me, [illegible] there [illegible]."

[illegible] I spoke [illegible]. They [illegible]

[illegible] back [illegible]

[illegible] you [illegible] you [illegible]

[illegible]

[illegible] the [illegible] the [illegible]

[illegible]

[illegible] and [illegible]

[illegible]

[illegible] the [illegible]

[illegible]

[illegible]

[illegible] and [illegible]

[illegible] on [illegible]

[illegible]

I [illegible] and showed the two deals into the [illegible] and [illegible] them down.

[illegible]

[illegible] the [illegible] and [illegible] the [illegible]

[illegible]

[illegible]

[illegible]

Chapter 26

Depression rolled over me like a two-ton tank. I won the hand, sure, even came out ahead, but I was depressed. The brownstones were a weight I couldn't throw off. Fate dealt me a rotten hand.

The rest of the players cleared. Harry settled up, and we sipped brandy in the wilds of Africa. For the first time I noticed the room. Decorated in a jungle motif, it was Harry's gambling den. Fake leopard skin patterned the walls. If you looked for too long a time you got dizzy. Elephant tusks and other animal horns adorned the walls, and I wondered what that was all about. Harry on safari? Anything was possible. You could never tell with Harry.

A well-stocked bar, a maroon couch, white leather chairs, and the leather-covered poker table filled the room to bursting. A bear rug, with head intact, lay on the floor in front of the couch. Next to it, a naked-lady floor lamp. A lightbulb crescendoed out of her head, and her gigantic titties blinked on and off and added to the décor. What can I say? The room was like Harry, tasteless and excessive.

I hadn't drunk all night, but Harry's brandy was mellow and I felt entitled.

"Ah well, next time you won't be so lucky," Harry said.

"Won't be a next time."

"Heard that before—from you, I think. And here you are."

Harry was right. Damn his eyes. Now that my gambling fever had dissipated, I acknowledged to myself that he was probably right when he said earlier that I was no better than him. I had put the lives of people I liked and lived with into a cutthroat drug dealer's hands, the very same dealer with whom I was now having a brandy, and had yet to feel remorse.

Instead, I felt empty. I had switched my feelings off altogether.

Harry studied me through the slits of his eyes and posed a philosophical question to me. "What are you looking for, Amos?"

The question struck me as odd, coming from Harry, but I gave him the courtesy of an answer. "What do you mean?" I said.

"Money, power, women, excitement—what is it that you want?"

The response hovered on the edge of my brain. I didn't have the words to answer Harry. And frankly, Harry was getting too chummy for me.

I settled for an answer that was, well, not untrue. "A comfortable life," I said. I didn't want to take it further. Wasn't Harry's business.

"Just comfortable? Hah. You ain't wantin' much. Me, the day I come to the United States, I want everything. Everything that growing up in the islands poor and wanting, I ain't never had."

"Take a look, Harry. You pretty much have it now, don't you?"

He smiled. "Not yet. Next thing, a plane. Anyway, that was when I was young. Since then I found out, it ain't about getting things. It's about glory. That's all it ever was. I want the glory. Look at me. Turned me-self into a somebody—him who was a nobody."

I stared at Harry.

"Ain't that what you want, Amos? Eh? I could make you somebody, you know. A hell of a somebody. No problem."

If I live to be a hundred, I'll never know what made me do it. Maybe it was the lack of sleep, or maybe it was Harry's snake eyes that hypnotized me, but I was lulled by his words to a place in my head where I had never been before. I thought hard about Harry's offer and told him I might be interested. The possibility of making a million a day seduced me like no woman could.

Harry smiled and nodded. "Come on, I want to show you something."

I followed the swaying cobra up to the third floor and down a hallway. We stopped in front of a closed door. Key in hand, Harry turned the lock.

"You got a handkerchief?" Harry asked. He didn't wait for my reply. "Use it," he said, and opened the door.

Puzzled, I got out my handkerchief and followed Harry into the room. Good God. Winter wonderland. I covered my nose and mouth the same as Harry.

In the center of the room were wide tables stacked with what must have been millions of dollars' worth of heroin. Standing next to the tables and chopping away like mad were seven naked women with surgical masks covering their faces. Vestal virgins? Not likely. Not the way Harry caressed the hind parts of the head woman he referred to as Peaches.

He had her ass in his beefy hand as he introduced me to her and her girls. Peaches didn't miss a beat and kept on whacking. Drifts of snow settled on the globes hanging from her chest. I looked around at the rest of the women. Dark nipples peeked from under the drifts like the mountains of Kilimanjaro and their pubic hair was frosty with fine powder. A regular Currier and Ives winter scene.

I tried to act as though it were an everyday thing, but with naked women standing around jiggling titties and chopping, it was a chore. The women continued their work as if Harry and I were invisible.

Harry turned out to be quite the tour director. He informed me the heroin was cut with 60 percent mannite and 40 percent quinine. The women weighed it and slipped it into plastic bags, ready for street sale. Harry grinned like a fat cat, but his asthma soon got the best of him and we ditched the room in a hurry.

Next Harry wanted to show off his ammo room. Guns, ammo, and even grenades filled closets and shelves. What I was about to get into got real to me in a hurry. A small fear turned around an axis in the pit of my stomach. Harry was a bona fide gangster with all the trappings. The tour over, we headed back down to Harry's private office.

"So, what you think, man?"

"Uh, impressive, Harry. Impressive."

"All that smack you see? Be gone in a week. Supply and demand, babe. And I make good profits 'cause I cut the Guineas out. This stuff comes straight from southeast Asia, the Golden Triangle—no middle man. Tragic Magic, me calls it, the best stuff out there—ten percent purity, no lie. Cleaned by a factory owned and operated by the CIA."

I raised my eyebrows at that. Harry nodded smugly, knowingly. "Would I lie?"

I didn't answer. Hell, at this moment, I didn't know what Harry was capable of. But I had no illusions about the CIA, either. Again, anything was possible.

"So much money you can make, man. Wave a bag on any street corner, and like cockroaches, junkies be swarming all over you, begging for it, ready to sell their souls for it. Any idea how rich I am?"

I had an idea, but I didn't share. I figured Harry would tell me anyway.

"I own four cars, three houses, a chain of dry cleaners, a grocery store, and a pool hall. Got money stashed in the Cayman Islands and two, three places around town. I got a bank in my pocket that launders money for me. I own furs, jewels, diamonds—and people. I own *people*, man. That's how rich I am."

"King of Harlem, huh, Harry?"

"Is right. Throw in with me, and you—hey, I'll let you be a duke, no lieutenant stuff for you. How's that? Have your own little turf. Sweet, eh?"

"All your boys are island boys, Harry."

"That's right, most of them relatives too. That's how I know I can trust them."

"So why are you making this offer to me? What exactly do I got to do to be a duke, Harry?"

He smirked at me like he knew a secret. "Well, you an almost relative. What you got to do? The name of the game is drugs, Amos. Drugs. I need people around me I can trust. Demand is overriding my supply. Got to expand. Like the CEOs downtown, you know?"

"What makes you think you can trust me?"

"I hear things. Bonus is, you smart. Plus I ain't crazy—gone give you a lil' test. You pass, you're in."

I dug my hands in my pocket, switched off any emotions that threatened to surface, and waited for Harry to explain.

Harry pushed a button under his desk and one of the Clots appeared. For the next half hour, Harry filled me in on what he expected. The *test* seemed easy, but risky. All I had to do was make a buy. One of the Clots was going to be my backup. I told Harry I was confused. I thought he told me he got his drugs straight from the Triangle.

"Yeah, well, this bundle done drop from heaven. A bargain, me think. Anyway, that's what you gone find out. Can we trust this somebody we dealing with, and can I trust you? Two mints in one, man." Harry chuckled at his joke, but I wasn't laughing.

If my plan was to self-destruct, this was sure the way to do it. I'd better have my own backup and a plan B.

Harry handed me a case filled with money. "They promised ten kilos. Tomorrow night, one A.M., East Harlem River at 135th Street under the bridge next to the expressway." Then Harry grinned. "If things turn funky, to come back with the drugs *and* the money, well, that would be a real fine thing. Play it like you see it."

He nodded to the Clot. "George there gone pick you up and take you there."

Hell no, I trusted George about as far as I could throw him. "If you don't mind, Harry, I'd rather take my own wheels. Trust runs both ways, and I'd feel easier, you know. I'll meet him there." I guess the Clot was insulted, 'cause he snorted like a bull, but I was letting Harry know he wasn't dealing with no fool. I planned to come out of it, no matter how the deal went down.

Harry smiled. "You the duke, it's up to you. Either way, gone find out if them are balls or cream puffs hanging between your legs."

Once again, I turned off my mind and let fate take the lead. I looked Harry in the eye and said, "One A.M., tomorrow." I hefted the case and walked. Harry's voice caught me at the door.

"You got a piece, man?"

"Not heavy artillery, Harry."

Harry pulled a 9mm from his desk drawer and handed it over to me. The gun sealed the deal.

Outside, the mugginess assaulted me. I felt its pressure on my chest. My face dripped sweat. I was in need of a cool, cleansing shower. And where was my fucking car when I needed it? Me, with a hundred thousand swinging off the end of my arm. For God's sake, fucking criminals were loose in these streets.

Chapter 27

Dawn leapfrogged over the Harlem skyline and was peeking through the buildings by the time I returned home. My dogs hurt and I didn't know money could weigh so much. I flung the briefcase across a folding chair in the office, opened a bottle of bourbon, and took a swig. I eased off my shoes and went to the window in my bare socks and gazed out.

I stood there for a long while, not really seeing anything. When the street lamps blinked off, it startled me and I became aware of the activity on the street.

With the first rays of dawn, the night people had melted back into their cracks and crevasses. But three young punks across the street, two with doo-rags tied around their heads, didn't move. They swarmed in the front of the basement entrance to my brownstone.

Instantly alert, I followed their actions. The smallest one, baseball cap on head, slid his hand through the iron bars and tapped on the window. It didn't take an Einstein to figure they were up to no good. Friends of Youngblood?

I backed up to the file cabinet where I had stashed my twenty-five. Forget Harry's piece; I was more comfortable with mine. I pulled the small weapon from the top drawer and returned to the window and stood watch.

A light snapped on inside Youngblood's apartment. The tallest boy knelt outside in front of the window. From underneath the security bars, a tray appeared. All three threw something into the tray and the contraption snapped shut and recoiled like a turtle. A minute later it reappeared, and the tallest boy dove for its contents and waved his catch in the air. Even at this distance I could tell they were plastic bags. The other two boys scrambled for the bags like dogs after a bone.

Motherfuck. Light shot through my head. A drug dealer selling out of my house. *My* house. Dizzy with rage, I thudded out of my door in my stocking feet and charged like a madman across the street, gun held high. Two of the punks ran like hell when they saw me. The small one wasn't as swift. He stumbled to his feet and froze, trapped. Frightened eyes peered from under his cap and focused on the gun pointed at his head. I stuffed the gun in my waistband, grabbed the little fucker by the collar, and shook him until his teeth rattled.

"No, don't, don't, Mr. Brown. Please."

What the—A girl? I knocked the cap off her head. Jesus. It was Patty, knees knocking, in front of me. Words wouldn't come, I was thunderstruck. She dived for her cap, seeking safety between the cracks of cement.

Suddenly, Youngblood shot out of the basement door with a gun aimed at me. I whirled and smacked the gun out of his hand and put all my weight behind a bone-crunching left hook. Youngblood toppled in a heap on the ground next to Patty. She scrambled backward like a crab. I retrieved Youngblood's gun and placed my foot on his neck.

I yelled at Patty to get her butt home. She hesitated, and I let out a roar and she bolted, across the street and swiftly up the brownstone's stairs. The door slammed behind her as I ground my heel deeper into Youngblood's neck and he screamed in pain.

Because my pain was just as deep I screamed back just as loud, "Didn't I tell you to keep your nose clean around here? *Didn't* I?"

He squealed like a pig, "Yes, ye-e-s."

"And you didn't, did you?" A shot to the ribs with my foot lifted his skinny ass off the ground.

"No-o," Youngblood blubbered.

"Well, that means you broke the terms of your lease, asshole.

Before the sun sets, you better have your drug-dealing butt out of this apartment and off this block. I never want to see your slimy face around here again."

I hauled him to his feet, propped him against the wall, and said, "You understand me?"

His head flopped on his scrawny neck, but he managed to squeak out a yes, and I let him drop like a sack of potatoes.

When he hit the ground I heard applause, and turned to see my neighbors gathered on stoops and in the street. Some were dressed, ready to go to work, others stood in underwear and bathrobes. They called out my name, raised their fists, and cheered, and applauded some more.

I can't tell you what that did to me. A ripple of shame shot through me. I couldn't look them in the eyes.

Embarrassed, I stepped over Youngblood's body, quickly crossed the street, and disappeared into my house.

My body shook and I couldn't control it. Emotion overcame me and I faced the desk and braced my body against it. This was as low as I had ever come. The accusing eyes in the photographs stared up at me. I was a hypocrite and a fool. I swung my gaze around at the suitcase full of money and groaned.

A knock on the door made me straighten. Wilbur swished into the room in a flowing red silk kimono. I swiped one hand across my eyes and lifted my head.

"What do you want, Wilbur?"

He took a moment to take me in and began tentatively, "I heard what happened. This is all my fault. I was the one told Patty to go out and have some fun."

"You didn't mean for her to do drugs, did you? And be out all hours of the morning with a two-year-old baby at home?"

"No, no, nothing like that. Believe me, I didn't know she was doing that. She was having a tough time, you know? I thought by watching Josie for her I would give her a little break. It's all my fault. I didn't think she would do what she did."

Wilbur was as upset as I was. I shook my head. "It's not your fault, Wilbur. Patty knew what she was doing."

"Yes, it is, Mr. B. See, the awful thing is, I knew she was hanging with that scuzz across the street, and I thought, well, he sure ain't my taste, but at least she had somebody to hang with, him being the same age and all. Honest, Mr. B., I didn't know the dog was dealing drugs."

I said, "I hope to God she ain't hooked. Turn into another one of these zombies that roam the streets."

Thinking about that possibility made us both quiet. Then Wilbur said, "Mr. B.?"

"What, Wilbur?"

"You ain't going to kick Patty out, are you? She don't have no place to go. She just made a mistake, a stupid mistake. It won't happen again."

I didn't respond. I was too weary to say anything. Too tired and too disgusted.

"Mr. B.?"

I sighed. "I'll talk to her in a couple of days. Go on, Wilbur."

"Oh, you bet, Mr. B. I'm going to ream her ass out. What she did was stupid. I'll see to it she stays as far away from drug dealers as she can possibly get."

Guilt made me choke and dip my head. "Don't promise the impossible, Wilbur."

"You get some rest, Mr. B."

"Right. Later, Wilbur."

"Tah, Mr. B." A swish and Wilbur was gone.

Now I had to face myself.

Chapter 28

Stewing in my own juices, and undecided on what action to take, I started in my chair when I heard scratching at the door. Silently I stood, crept to the door, slung it open, and caught Zeke, red-handed, with one of his voodoo bags. I snagged him by the collar and pulled him into the room.

"For protection, for protection . . ." he stuttered. Zeke looked like a cornered rat.

"What the devil are you doing, and what were you doing last night?"

"I told you, protection. Obvious you have need of it."

A peculiar smell emanated from Zeke's clothes—a cloying, sickly odor. I sniffed the air and asked, "What's that smell?"

Zeke's face darkened and he brushed his hands together and replied, "Coffee."

Well, it didn't smell like coffee to me, but I let it pass. "Take a seat, Zeke, we need to talk and clear the air."

Trapped, Zeke sat down on the rickety folding chair. I didn't tell him to take that seat—he was just determined to be uncomfortable. I handed him a steaming cup of coffee—coffee that smelled like coffee, I might add—and he accepted it.

Diplomacy oozed from my pores, and I took a breath and said, "You and me have gotten off on the wrong foot, Zeke, and I'd like to mend that rift." No response.

"Okay then, have it your way, but we can at least be civil. We're grown men, and this stuff is childish." I leaned forward in my seat. "My mother's body was buried in a basement wall nearly thirty-eight years ago. You and my father were best friends. I know that." I showed him the "friends to the end" photo. "See, I got pictures." Zeke stared at it. "What the hell happened, Zeke?"

Zeke's scowl deepened. He didn't respond right away and bought time by slurping his coffee, which got on my nerves, and then he got up and walked to the window and looked out.

After a time he spoke. "I come to this country a young man, forty-five years ago. Life was hard then. In Trinidad I worked in the cane field, had a steel band. But no, not enough—not enough for me."

Shades of Harry. Zeke's history was not unique. In the twenties and thirties Harlem attracted blacks from inside and outside this country like a magnet. Zeke paused and I urged him on. "So?"

"Find a better life here, I thought. More money, live like king. Traded the beaches, turquoise sea, white sands . . . for Harlem. In Trinidad a man could pluck he dinner from the ocean, he dessert from tree—a paradise. You ain't know what that's like."

Zeke sounded homesick. The rhythms alternated in his speech—now an American inflection, now West Indian, as he slipped from culture to culture with subconscious ease. I nodded. "I can imagine, Zeke. I can imagine."

"Montcrieff came from the South. Alabama. Same time. We meet. Two young men in strange place, big dreams . . . become brothers, you know, help each other out, share everything. Then—what happen? We grow apart, want different things. He go right. Me, I find the Left Path." He turned back to me. "Understand?"

I thought I understood. I murmured, "Sure, the left path . . . But your agreement with Montcrieff—tell me, what 'services' did you render in lieu of paying rent?"

Anger choked Zeke's throat, his eyes darkened, and he turned to face me. "Montcrieff and me buy houses, same time almost. Black people don't own houses in Harlem—but we do. Kings then. Then poof, go up in smoke—hard times. I lose mine. Montcrieff work the railroads, a steady job, bought up mortgage, promised to hold it for me, until I could pay him back."

I shook my head. "Still don't understand, Zeke. What was it that you did for *him*?"

Zeke smiled an awful smile. "I gave him something, something valuable, something he wanted. Is too bad he couldn't hang on to it. In case of his death, agreement says property comes back to me."

I sat up straight in my seat. "That's what Part Two of the agreement means? That the property would revert to you on his death?"

Zeke didn't say anything, but the muscles on his thin frame rippled, his anger evident. I laughed. "So that's why you're upset with me? I own something that you think belongs to you? Obviously, Montcrieff changed his mind."

I strode over to the closet, lifted a strongbox from off the shelf, and opened it with a skeleton key I took from my desk drawer. I pulled out Montcrieff's will and handed it to him, and showed Zeke the date printed at the top of the document.

"The will was revised several times over the years, but this trust document"—and I showed him that—"along with the will listed me as beneficiary ever since I was . . . let's see, seven years old. It cancels out the agreement with you. Sorry, Zeke, Montcrieff never intended to leave that property to you."

Zeke slammed his cup down on top of Montcrieff's bureau so hard the coffee sloshed over. "Montcrieff a lying viper."

"Can't argue with that. But tell you what, Zeke. I'll honor the agreement, the rent-free part, because Montcrieff obviously did." And then I looked at Zeke closely and asked the $64,000 question. "You think Montcrieff was viper enough to kill my mother?"

Zeke's eyes brightened and did that weird thing they did, and he spat out, "Yes, oh yes—your father killed your mother. With he bare hands, he murdered she. This is fact. And you, his progeny, are cursed because of it."

Not much to say after that. We stared at each other. The expression on Zeke's face sent a shiver through me—the hairs on the back of my neck lifted.

He left the room, an icy chill blew in, and left me numb from head to foot.

Chapter 29

Bam-bam-bam. Showing no mercy, someone pounded hard against the office door and rattled its hinges. What the hell? I glanced at the clock. Eleven-thirty. "Stop that noise and come in," I shouted, and Seltzer burst through with a jet stream up his ass.

"What's the matter with you, banging on the door like that, you little cockroach? What do you want?" I said.

"World done gone plumb out of its mind? Took my dog Susie to the vet, that's how come I'm just now getting here. What's this I hear about Patty?"

"You never saw Youngblood's contraption in the window?"

"What contraption?"

"Exactly what I'm saying."

"Guess I can throw the same question at you. How come you ain't seen it? You the one with young eyes. And by the way, you look like pure shit."

I felt like it too, and Seltzer picked up on that. But it didn't stop the barrage of questions.

"And what's going on with these for-sale signs all over the place? I ripped the dang things up. You ain't serious, is you? Huh, upset about your mama, I reckon. But look here, Montcrieff ain't leave you these houses for you to be selling 'em."

That did it. I exploded out of my chair, and it skidded backward and toppled over. "I don't give a shit about Montcrieff. I ain't never given a shit about him. And he never gave a shit about me. Montcrieff left me these houses to ease his fucking conscience, that's all. It wasn't about me. It never was about me." I was calling the cows home and I didn't care who heard me.

Seltzer had stepped into the eye of a hurricane and he didn't have a clue. He backed away from the heat.

"What you saying, Amos?"

Angrily, I shuffled papers around on my desk. I waited until the thumping in my chest subsided before I answered.

"It's payback, don't you see? Payback for taking my mother from me thirty-eight years ago. My own father killed my mother. Ain't that a legacy? Living under his roof makes my skin crawl." I tossed Montcrieff's photos, like Frisbees, in the wastebasket.

Seltzer watched and said softly, "Montcrieff done a lot of devilment in his time, he wasn't no perfect man, but I can't never think he'd do something like that, Amos, and I knowed him a long time."

Then he transferred the cap he held in his hand into a back pocket and picked through the wastebasket to retrieve the pictures. I told him it was good to be loyal, but to let it go.

"Naw, naw . . . ain't loyalty that be making me move my lips to speak for him. He ain't done what you say. Why you think he ain't never married again?"

"Guilt." I moved to pick up the chair where it had fallen.

"Why you think he fooled around with whores and the like?"

"Guilt. And because he was a pervert. And whores weren't the only women he fooled with. Did you know he had an affair with Miss Ellie?"

Seltzer's head dropped into his chest. Jesus. Everybody around here knew more than me about my parents. He said, "Didn't mean nothing. Ain't no one could replace your mama. He loved her, I'd bet my life on it."

"Necks been broke in the name of love. My mother's was. I don't have to remind you where she was found."

"Didn't have to be Montcrieff. Coulda been anybody. Coulda been your aunt Reba, wouldn't put it past her. I ain't never liked the woman."

I glanced at him, a question in my eyes.

"Your mother and Reba battled like crazy before your mother

disappeared. Didn't know what that was about, not my business, but I knew they had a feud."

I didn't reply right away, but wheels began to turn. What Miss Ellie had said . . . "You think the fight was over Montcrieff?"

Seltzer just looked at me. "All I can say is, it don't sound like Montcrieff. He tried to do right by people—tried to do right by you. Had to swallow his pride to do what he did."

I glared at Seltzer. "Enough about Montcrieff." I cut the discussion and said, "Selz, I need help."

I began with once upon a time, but cut quickly to the chase. Seltzer immediately got interested, removed the briefcase off the seat, and sat. When I finished telling about the whole episode with Harry, Seltzer couldn't contain himself. He took his cap from his back pocket and whammed me upside my head. It shocked the shit out of me. I snatched it away from him, but not before he had whopped me a couple more times.

"*Enough*," I said. "I admit I did something foolish. Now what?"

"You return that money to Harry Algonquin Bridges as fast as you can, that's what."

"Not that simple. The buy is tonight. Harry is in New Jersey, and Stepchild ain't running."

Thank God Seltzer was a man of action. We were on our way to New Jersey in Seltzer's machine. It was so raggedy that air blew up from a rotted-out hole in the floor. I saw the street whizz by between my two feet.

Seltzer and I made it halfway across the George Washington Bridge before it came to me, I had no idea in hell where Harry lived. When I told Seltzer he made a U-turn on the bridge and I lost a little water. I finally convinced him that going against traffic on a bridge was not a good idea and he made another U-ee, tires screeching, and we continued on to Englewood, home of Harry Algonquin Bridges.

Chapter 30

When we got to Englewood, I told Selz to head for the hills. Harry was probably there, or so my powers of deduction led me to believe. The rich always live in the hills or next to water. The really rich live in hills surrounded by water—on their own fucking island. It's about seclusion. Harry was rich so he had to be living in the hills, never mind that he was a drug king-pin or the wrong color.

Money was the great equalizer, so who the hell cared if Harry lived there? Not his neighbors. Being rich and secluded guaranteed that the neighbors didn't know beans about Harry. I should pass out leaflets.

To call Catherine and ask where Harry lived wasn't an option. Harry's inner circle would know, but that's why they were *inner*—they wouldn't tell an *outer* like me. No, better to cruise the hills and track Harry down by his cars. Look for that flashy gold Cadillac of his with the vanity tags, or the black limo in which he had meetings, or the red jaguar with the leopard seats, or his incognito car, which everyone in Harlem knew about—the blue Pinto. Harry used to sit in that Pinto, parked on Lenox Avenue and keep an eye on the drug buys. Minding the store, that's what he was doing.

Me, I assumed Harry couldn't park all those cars in one garage, right? They'd be out where I could see them, on the street or in the driveway. Wrong. How was I supposed to know that Englewood folks had four-car garages and lived behind gated walls?

And the number of houses with rich people in them, you wouldn't believe. The Englewood hills were overrun with them—as Seltzer and me soon found out. Huh, I'd bet my watch some of those upstanding citizens were as big a crook as Harry.

We cruised the streets for over an hour, looking. In mansion territory, the homes had electronic gates and high walls in front. Seclusion. It made the task of spotting Harry's cars difficult, to say the least. After Seltzer called me a fool for the tenth time, I told him to shut the fuck up.

We traveled at a snail's pace, me eyeballing each house, my body hung halfway out of the car.

"Give me a sign, a clue, anything," I shouted to the passing houses. Wouldn't you know, that's when I spotted it. A huge lavender mansion sheltered behind ten-foot walls and an electric gate at the entrance. The Arranger was listening.

I yelled at Seltzer to stop the car. The idiot braked, and I almost fell out. I glared at him, and then looked back at the gate. Molded across the top was a large crown, about the size of Harry's ego, and the words, "King Harry's Castle." See what I'm saying? What were the odds of that?

"Bingo." I smiled.

But no sooner had Seltzer and me scrambled out of the car than a New Jersey black-and-white showed, and rolled up behind us, lights flashing. The unlocked briefcase, chunk full of money, sat big as all get out on the back seat of Seltzer's car, and I started to sweat.

Two giddy-up cops with identical mustaches and hands touching their holsters strode towards us. Oh man, deep in the brown stuff now.

"What you boys up to? Been following you for the last fifteen minutes."

Seltzer's age and mine probably totaled five times both those cops' ages, but then wasn't the time to get rankled by cops calling us boys. Had to tread lightly. Wasn't even on my own turf. Before I had time to pull together an answer, Seltzer began acting like a bona fide fool, and did the best Step-n'-Fetchit imitation that I had ever had the displeasure to see. He plastered a grin across his face and acted like he was greeting his two best friends.

"Howdy, officers. Doing a job for somebody up here, and dang it, if we ain't left the address at home. All these places look alike, don't-cha know."

The cops looked at each other. "Let's see some I.D. Who you working for?"

"Uh, uh, Peter, Porter, uh . . ." Seltzer scratched his head and peeled his lips back like a baboon.

I couldn't take it any more, and jumped in, "Bridges, we're looking for a Mister Harry Bridges." I handed over my identification.

The cop with the red mustache glanced toward his partner. A silent exchange passed between them. Harry's name triggered something. Their eyes turned mean. Something told me I had made a big mistake.

The cop sneered, "Bridges, huh. What kind of work you doing for him?" This wasn't going too good. He strolled over and peered into Seltzer's car. My stomach flipped.

I took a few steps forward and the other cop stopped me. "Hold it right there," he said.

Seltzer chimed in, "Fix-it work, officer. Repairs."

The two cops ignored Seltzer and focused on me. Red Mustache said, "You don't look like you'd know the right end of a hammer. Looks more like a drug dealer, don't he, Sal?" He turned to the other cop and the other mustache grunted.

So much for my Brooks Brothers' shirt and slacks. I tried not to show I was nervous, but sweat rolled down into the crack of my butt. I took a cue from Seltzer, grinned like a motherfucker. Whatever worked. I dismissed the briefcase with a wave of my hand, "Contracts, work orders," and I took a step toward the trunk of the car and pointed. "Tools in there. Want to see?"

Uncertain, the two cops stood there. Finally, Red Mustache gestured to Seltzer, "You, open the trunk." Seltzer scurried to comply.

Seltzer had everything but the kitchen sink crammed in his trunk. I wasn't disappointed, but the cops were. Red Mustache looked at his partner, and pointed to a stereo sitting alongside a bunch of tools. "What's this?"

"That? Ain't nothing but an old stereo I been trying to get working," said Seltzer.

The cops looked skeptical. Red Mustache said to his partner, "Run a make on the car."

It was Seltzer's turn to sweat. I looked at him, curious, wondering what secret he harbored. Red Mustache instructed us to take a seat on the curb.

We sat and waited for a half an hour. Whatever news came across their radio, they pulled out handcuffs to haul us to the nearest station house. Visions of my balls being served up on a platter by Harry made me try to talk them out of it, but they didn't listen.

Seltzer pleaded with them to let him lock up the car. I didn't want to call attention to the briefcase, so I said nothing. I hoped Seltzer had enough smarts to slide the briefcase to the floor, at least. I watched him while they cuffed me. He looked like he did it. Off to the pokey we went.

Seltzer and I were silent during the ride.

I hadn't been in an interrogation room in years. Believe me, it wasn't something I missed. My anxiety level rose, but for a different reason. I sweated bullets about the money left in Seltzer's car, and about the one o'clock meet. I wondered if they would keep us all night.

They put Seltzer and me in separate rooms and leaned on me hard. Asked all kinds of questions about Harry, for God's sake, which didn't have anything to do with the robbery I was supposed to have committed. I claimed ignorance and stuck to it. It wasn't the hardest thing I ever did. They had nothing on me. I knew it and they knew it. My juvenile record was sealed, and my record was clean as far as they knew. They didn't like it, but they finally had to let me go.

I worried about Seltzer, though. He had a temper that wouldn't quit if you got him riled, and I wondered if they were sweating him. Released at nine o'clock that night, I got my answer. Seltzer waited outside. He didn't need to say a word. I could tell by the bruise on his face and the look in his eyes that they had been rough on him.

We hurried through the streets looking for a taxi. New Jersey taxis flew past us the same way taxis in New York City did. I held money in the air and finally one stopped. A brother was driving.

We jumped in and told him to take us back to Harry's. I gave him the address and prayed the money would be there.

On the way, Seltzer let it be known about his priors—two assaults. I raised my eyebrows.

He said, "When you're a small man, people tend to pick on you. I had to let some people know they couldn't do that."

I nodded. I understood. "You're a member of a large club—Kappa Kappa Jailbird, the black man's fraternity." We slapped hands.

After a few minutes, he added, "And the robbery charge against me was bogus. I was never convicted."

Now I wondered. Then when Seltzer started up again, talking about an indecent exposure arrest, I shut him up. The cab driver darted nervous glances back at us in his rearview mirror. I said to Seltzer, "Look, you don't have to explain. I ain't blaming you, man. I was the one got you mixed up in this."

Seltzer and I rode in silence the rest of the way. Seltzer kept touching the bruise on his face. I felt guilty as hell.

When the taxi rolled up to a stop in front of Harry's lavender mansion, I clutched my chest to keep my heart from dropping to my knees. The car was gone. Gone.

ACKNOWLEDGMENTS

[illegible]

[illegible]

[illegible]

[illegible]

[illegible]

[illegible]

[illegible]

Chapter 31

Seltzer tore out of the cab and ran around in circles, flapping his wings, screaming about his missing tools to a street lamp. I charged after him, wrestled with him for a minute, and then grabbed the little runt by his lapels and hissed a reminder in his ear, "The money, fool, the money. A hundred thousand *dollars*."

His hysteria stopped as quickly as it started. "Oh yeah," he said. I dragged him back into the cab, and we huffed and puffed in the back seat. What was there to say? The cabbie looked at us through his mirror as he munched on a sandwich. "Dinner. No time to eat. Is there a problem?" he said.

I let him know our transpo had sort of, well, disappeared.

"Ought to pay attention to signs, my brother." He indicated a NO PARKING sign illuminated by the gate lights of Harry's pad. "They done towed your ride," he said.

I thumped my head several times against the front seat. Could my luck get any worse? "Where would they have towed it to?"

"Outside the city."

"Can you take us there?"

"This time of night? Ain't nobody there."

"Good," I said. "We don't need for nobody to be there."

Seltzer said, "But—"

I silenced him with a look.

"Aww, naw, mister," the cabbie said. "I ain't up for no hanky-panky. I make an honest living. Driving a cab, that's all I do."

"That's all I want you to do, son." I flashed a hundred-dollar bill at him.

Seltzer mumbled to himself. The cabbie ran a finger around his collar that had suddenly gotten too tight for him. "Uh, uh . . . well . . ."

"Just take us there. You don't have to do anything else. What do you say?"

His nervous eyes shifted back and forth. "Uh, uh, okay."

I looked at my watch. Time was whipping by. It was eleven-fucking-thirty.

"Let's ride," I ordered. Seltzer's protest was muffled by the screech of tires as the cab rocketed away. He shouted, "You crazy as a bed-bug, Amos Brown."

"I heard that, Seltzer."

"I meant for you to, ya damn fool."

I looked at him and back at my watch. Eleven thirty-three and counting.

Chapter 32

The barbed wire at the top of the chain-link fence gave me a little something to think about, but the Dobermans guarding the yard stopped me cold. They looked vicious. Where I figured the office to be was dark. The yard was lit up like Christmas, and Seltzer and me stood outside the front gate, exposed and vulnerable. I was ready to give it up and proceed to plan B, but Seltzer talked me out of it. Besides, we didn't have a plan A, so plan B was a joke.

Seltzer conversed in doggie-talk with the two mutts and, what do you know, the dogs stopped yapping. Seltzer cooed, "Nice doggies" to the both of them, and tried to squeeze his hand through the padlocked gates to pet the pooches. The dumb shit. They growled deep in their throats and I jerked his ass away.

We circled the perimeter as far as we were able. At the rear of the yard was a small building and a large carport. Along the side of the fence where the wire ended and the concrete wall began was a space—big enough, maybe, to climb through and over the top. Maybe. It had been a while since I had scaled any fences.

Seltzer spotted his raggedy Buick, sitting in the first row of cars, next to a Benz. Equality—what I liked to see. The yard was filled with all kinds of cars. The dust on some of them looked like they'd sat there for months. Selz and me rapidly concocted a plan. It was iffy, but there was no alternative, and hey, I was good to go.

We trotted back to the waiting cab. Brother-Man the cabdriver was nervous as a cat. I didn't blame him. He wasn't by himself. We snatched his sandwich out of his mouth and his lunch off the seat, and Seltzer asked him if he had a blanket or something stashed in the trunk. "Or something" turned out to be a padded mat. Good. Our luck had improved. About time.

Seltzer returned to the front gate, did his doggie thing again, and slipped grapes to the mutts and what was left of Brother-Man's sandwich. I jogged back to the side of the fence where I had seen an opening and scaled it, the mat thrown over my shoulder.

When I reached the top, I doubled the mat, laid it across part of the prickly wire, and then eased myself over. Should I leave the mat for a swift retreat? I looked to where the dogs were. Naw. I dropped to the ground and took it with me.

I passed swiftly along the row of cars until I reached Seltzer's heap. The dogs started up their barking again. I turned back. Uh-oh. They were tearing across the yard, heading for me. I fumbled in my pocket for Seltzer's keys as the dogs bounded closer. I unlocked the door, flung it open. The dogs leaped through the air to attack. I dove inside and pulled the door shut, in the nick, as they say, and the mutts slammed into the side of the car.

I clipped one, and he yelped and tumbled backward on top of the other. You think that stopped them? Both hounds recovered quickly and scrambled to their feet and lunged again. I thumbed my nose at them. That made them madder, and they barked and threw themselves repeatedly against the side of the car. The car rocked like a cradle. I was sweating. I threw the blanket off me, and told myself to think. *Think.*

Thud. Bump. The shocks were catching hell. I climbed over the front seat and pawed through the junk in the back.

Thud. Bump. Thud. Bump.

The briefcase wasn't there. I panicked. My fingers dipped into something sticky. Damn. Junk flew. Time was short.

Outside, between leaps, the dogs' barks turned to howls. I gave up. No use. The briefcase was not there. I almost wept.

I looked through the car window. Seltzer had come around and was standing outside the fence hollering and waving at me. I rolled down the window an inch or two. The dogs lunged with renewed viciousness.

Again, he shouted something, but I couldn't hear because of the damn dogs.

"What?" I screamed.

He pantomimed and made an O with his right hand, and with his left index finger jabbed it in and out of the hole. Was he trying to say, "Screw me"?

"Hole, hole," he screamed. I finally caught it.

Hole. I looked down. Sure enough, there was a tear in the upholstery across the bottom of the back seat. I slid my hand through and, hot-cha-cha, touched the handle of the briefcase.

I tugged, and out it came, tearing away more of the upholstery. I checked to see if the money was there. It was. I breathed a sigh of relief.

I looked out at the dogs. Foam dripped from their mouths. How would I get out of the car without being eaten alive?

The cabbie sprinted over to Seltzer and screamed, "The cops. The cops are coming," and pointed off in the distance. Him I heard. I had to get my butt out of there. No time to think. I jumped into the driver's seat, turned on the ignition, hit the pedal, and aimed the car for the front gates.

Ker-boom. I plowed into them and my head butted against the windshield. The glass didn't break, but my head did. Blood trickled down into my eyes. I was dizzy. And the damn locks didn't pop like I expected, but I had succeeded in getting the gates to buckle—maybe enough to squeeze through the top of the bent gate.

Did I lose the dogs? Hell no. They chased after the car, barking louder. I whipped off my belt, wrapped the mat twice around me, and secured it with the belt. While the dogs tried to rip my arm off, I opened the car window, pushed the briefcase up and onto the roof.

I opened the door a fraction, then wham, kicked the door hard into the jumping dogs. They flew backward, and I made it to the roof of the car—almost. One hound from hell charged at my backside. I kicked at him, the mat barely offering protection, and struggled to pull myself to the roof. He caught my pant leg and hung on. I was beltless and my pants were being pulled halfway down my ass.

Seltzer and the cabbie screamed. This was insane. I managed to half sit on the roof of the car. I hurled the briefcase over the gate to Seltzer, and yelled to Brother-Man to start his cab. With the dog hanging on to my pant leg, I squeezed through the opening in the gate, got stuck halfway. Seltzer yanked from the other side and pulled me the rest of the way through. The jerk made the hound from hell let go of my pant leg and the dog skidded off the car, and took half of my pant leg with him.

The sirens loomed closer.

"Let's get to getting," I shouted.

The taxi was already rolling when Seltzer and me jumped into it. Tires squealed as we tore out of there. Two blocks down the street we almost crashed into the black-and-white that careened around the corner. The cabdriver gave the finger to the cops and yelled obscenities. The cops ignored him and roared past, sirens wailing. I gave Brother-Man a look of admiration.

"Offensive tactics. Where to?" he said, grinning.

I looked at my watch. Twelve forty-five.

"Harlem. Floor it." I stuffed a hundred-dollar bill in his unused ashtray and waved another hundred under his nose.

"A hundred and thirty-fifth Street and Harlem River Drive."

He smiled again and put pedal to metal; the speedometer soared. The old cab shook as we boogied through the night.

Chapter 33

We were late by five minutes. The taxi parked one block over. Brother-Man promised to wait for twenty minutes. Any time after that, he said, we were on our own. The moon shone foolishly. A limp summer breeze carried the smell of ripe garbage and the Harlem River to our nostrils.

I moved like a wooden puppet across the deserted expanse of street; muscles coiled, my body resisted each step of the way. Deep within I knew I didn't want to do this, but still, like a robot, I laid one foot after the other, Seltzer at my side. We headed for the underpass and, I knew, straight into the mouth of hell.

As we approached the meeting place, I slowed, peered into the darkness ahead, and listened. I heard the hum of a car's engine and stopped.

Seltzer asked, "What is it, boss?"

Through the gloom I saw the outline of two cars parked fifty feet from each other, headlights off. The shape of the second car disturbed me. It had an official look to it. "Trouble, I think."

"My knife's back at the station house. Boss, you got a gun?"

Seltzer's question hit me like a bullet to my brain.

The guns were stashed back at the office, and no help to us here. I froze. The doors on the car to my right opened. Two white guys climbed out, one short, one tall.

I pegged them immediately as cops. *Cops*. What had I got myself into? I backed up slowly and whispered to Seltzer, "How fast can you run?"

Before we could take off, the tall one whipped out a big-dick gun and said, "Hold it." Jesus. If I were Catholic, this was sure enough the time to start saying Hail Marys.

A loud bang sounded off to my left, and I flinched, thinking I was being shot at. Two men exploded out of the second car. For the first time ever, I was happy to see Blood Clot. But who in the hell was that with him?

Nooo . . . Zeke? Zeke? I was stunned. Seltzer clawed at my arm. He was as surprised as I was. What the devil was Zeke doing here?

Clot approached, his hands wrapped around a junior cannon pointed at the cops. Zeke trailed and pulled something from the bag he carried. A gun, too? Surprise, he threw dust in the air and scattered some on the ground in front of the cops. Then he waved his hand around and started jabbering that geechie West Indian shit.

I muttered between my teeth, "Zeke and his damned voodoo." I cut my eyes at Seltzer and back at Zeke. This was unreal. Zeke was a cuckoo bird of the first order.

The tall cop went ballistic. "What the fuck is this shit? Where is Harry?" And he looked me up and down.

"Who is Harry?" I asked.

"Don't get cute on me," the cop said. He was agitated. Maybe Zeke's business had spooked him. "You got the money?"

A forgotten childhood ditty surfaced. "I got the money. I got the time. Let's get together and drink some wine." Stress made me say it.

The cops looked at me as if *I* were crazy. One of them looked me up and down and asked, "What's with the raggedy pants?"

I didn't bat an eye. "A disguise."

"You aren't who I expected," he said.

I said, "No shit, Snowflake, that makes two of us. Ain't dealing with no cops."

The two looked at each other. The tall one said, "We aren't cops."

Seltzer busted out laughing; I followed suit. Clot and Zeke joined in. Pretty soon we were all pretty much hysterical. A Kodak moment. Even in the dark, the two cops' cheeks glowed bright red.

The short one cut us off. "Not NYPD, okay? You do business with us, there's more where this came from. Much as you can handle, and on a regular basis. What do you say?"

That's when it hit me. Of course. The bad haircuts. They had to be DEA with recycled dope. Wouldn't it be funny if the dope was Harry's?

Well, well, well . . . DEA pretzel turds, bent and twisted. I had another sudden thought that made me dizzy. Was this where my tax dollars went? Wasn't someone in an office somewhere supposed to keep track of this dope? I was indignant.

"No," I said loudly and walked away. The tall one fired. Clot reacted and let go a round and three people hit the deck. I didn't know if they had been shot or not.

Tall One screamed, "What do you mean no? Who do you think you are? You're taking this smack with you, you dumb shit."

"No," I said.

"No?" said Clot, the question dotting his eyes. Then he trained his gun on me too. Great.

"No," I repeated. I couldn't help it. I was mad.

The tall one snatched the dope out of his partner's hand and came for me, and I'm not proud of this, he wound up and smacked me—wham—right in the kisser. I was thrown off balance and fell on my butt. Smacked with smack. Then he lunged for the briefcase and tried to take it away from me. Seltzer leaped on his back. Tall One's partner and Clot charged and jumped in, and the brawl began.

A caravan of trucks rumbled overhead—and we rumbled below. Zeke disappeared. I think he went and sat in the car.

After only five minutes of fighting I was pooped. The cut opened above my eye again, and blood dotted my shirt—my good shirt. Clot lay knocked out on the ground. Short One held a gun to Seltzer's ear. Sucking in air and breathing hard, Tall One said, "It doesn't have to be this difficult, understand? Two weeks from today. Same time, same place. Ten kilos delivered. Play ball, and we'll all be rich."

Me, I didn't like the way they played. I wasn't having fun. Tall One picked up the briefcase, shoved the dope at me, and him and his partner split.

I looked at Clot's motionless body. What kind of bodyguard was he? I left him knocked out, on the ground. Let Zeke and his voodoo take care of him.

Seltzer said, "If I'da had my knife, I'da cut him."

I dusted the dirt and garbage off my pants and said, "If-Ida was a good horse, Selz, but she ran too late." I reluctantly picked up the bag of heroin. I added, "It's a good thing you *didn't* have your knife."

When we got back to the street where Brother-Man had parked his taxi, it had disappeared. He probably split about the same time the gunshots exploded. Who could blame him? Seltzer and me walked the distance back to my place. Me, with one million dollars' worth of heroin slung over my shoulder.

Chapter 34

I slept for twelve hours. When my eyes popped open, it was mid-afternoon of the next day. The first thing I saw was the duffel bag of heroin—it eyed me accusingly from the corner of the room. I pulled the sheet back over my head and pretended the bag wasn't there.

Hell, I pretended *I* wasn't there, and tried to fantasize myself on an island in the Bahamas somewhere. But I wasn't getting good reception on that picture. My muscles ached too much. Wild imaginings crowded my brain.

Sounds of the living flowed around me like a never-ending river. Doors banged, telephones rang, and Miss Winnie tripped back and forth above me, the floor creaking under her bulk.

Seltzer's last shot before he left was, "What're you gonna do now, boss?"

Did I know?

I groaned and pushed myself out of the bed. Wandering into the living room, I found a note from Seltzer on the coffee table with my car keys on top. It read *Kar fist.* Took me a minute, but I translated that to mean that he had rescued Stepchild and fixed the carburetor. Good old Selz.

I jumped in the shower and stood for twenty minutes, my head and hands pressed against the cold tiles in front of me, the water rushing down my neck. Images clattered through my head like stills on a slide projector. I pictured my mother, the way I had when I was young, which was nowhere close to reality—a beautiful white angel goddess who watched over me. Me, with a black daddy and a black mama, and still, in my mind she was white. Well, hell, weren't all angels white? Was she watching now?

The image of her in her wedding photo flashed in my mind. And then Montcrieff's face cascaded through, his face angry and threatening, and the picture became a moving one. His fists smashed into my mother's face and body. She broke away. He grabbed her by the hair and knocked her to the floor. Her body lay silent and still.

And then the thought of her body, hanging half out of a basement wall, made me press my fingers to my eyes, to force the image away, but her body kept dropping to the floor in an unending loop of repeated action—and Montcrieff struggled to plaster it into the wall.

I beat my hands against the tile to stop the pictures, then grabbed a bar of soap and fiercely lathered my body. Hand sudsing my joint, I forced my eyes open and confronted the present. That voodoo shit, did Zeke have any brain cells left? What in the hell was he doing there last night? Did Harry know? Of course he did.

What was I going to do? I hadn't been born stupid—but I had done some stupid shit in the last couple of days. Like I was under some spell. Spell. I jerked my head up, and hit the damn shower head. Electric pain zapped my body. The bar of soap shot out of my hand. Motherfuck. I bent down to retrieve the soap, and my right foot slid on the soap scud at the bottom of the tub. I grabbed at the shower curtain, and the whole damn thing tumbled down.

Ain't that the shits? To end it all by cracking my skull on the edge of a tub. A piss-poor way to exit this world. I held on to the sides of the tub and balanced like a surfer riding the waves. After a few seconds I let go, and that's when the idea formed about what I should do. To hell with Harry. He wasn't going to use me to pollute Harlem. First, I'd return the smack to the cops.

I climbed out of the tub, slapped a bandaid on the cut over my eye, and decorated the nicks and scrapes on the rest of my body with mercurochrome. Those mutts at the impound lot—did they have rabies? I hoped not, but I'd have to take my chances.

Life, ain't it all about chance? Okay, my turn to roll the dice.

Dressing, I whistled a few bars of the old Negro spiritual "Nobody Knows de Trouble I've Seen," and that cheered me some.

An hour later I climbed the stairs to Bundt's office at the Twenty-eighth Precinct and laid the duffel bag across his desk.

Chapter 35

Bundt took one look, went ballistic, and hustled me and the heroin out into the hallway. Grabbing me by the collar, he pushed his face close to mine. "What the hell, Brown? What are you doing? Are you crazy? Where'd you get this?"

"I, uh, found it."

"In a pig's eye."

"What difference does it make? I'm turning it in. You should be happy."

"Bringing me a load of shit? DEA stamped? You think that makes me happy?" His voice rose to a shout, and his ears turned a bright pink.

"Brown, I ain't happy. Do I look happy? I ain't taking this."

His partner, Caporelli, chose that moment to nosy into the hall, and he called from the doorway, "What's going on, Bundt? Need some help?"

Bundt released his grip on me. "Naw, it's all right, Cap, I can handle it." He thumped me on the shoulder and flicked an imaginary piece of lint off my chest. "Grief has made Mr. Brown here a little crazy, but he's better now, aren't you, Mr. Brown?"

I muttered, "What's the matter? Can't trust your partner?"

"No," Bundt squeezed out, "he's more tight-assed than me. *He* might arrest you—ever think of that?"

"For doing my civic duty?" I asked.

Bundt hit the roof. On the float down he said, "How about for possession, Brown? What the fuck do you got up there for brains?" He emphasized his point by thumping me on my forehead with his meaty index finger. Unnecessary; I got it.

Bundt scooped up the bag that lay on the floor between us and slammed it into my gut. With the wind knocked out of me, it was hard to protest, but I tried. I got out one "But—" before Bundt interrupted.

"Look, numb-nuts, I'm doing you a favor. Pay attention. I don't care what you do with that heroin, but you get rid of it—pronto. I ain't touching it. I'm not getting mixed up with the feds and tanking my career for you. Homicide, that's what I'm paid to do, and that's what I do. When you find another dead body, call me."

On the street and around the corner I could take him. It'd be no contest. Here was another story, some inhibiting factors, like about two hundred cops to one of me. Caporelli stood watching, smoking a cigarette.

"You find my mother's killer?" I said. His eyes turned evil and his head swung around almost like the child's in *The Exorcist*—a movie I had seen recently. Bundt moved away and left me standing in the hallway, holding the bag.

Nothing left to do, so I walked out of the precinct, like Santa Claus at Christmastime, with the bag over my shoulder, past a dozen cops and detectives coming in and going out of the building. No one even bothered to look my way, except for two men with fucked-up haircuts that I passed at the foot of the stairs, one short, one tall.

Awww, no. What were the odds? I trekked fast, fast, fast, and hustled to the precinct's front door and sped like a bullet to my car. I snatched open Stepchild's door and threw the heroin into the back seat. Tires squealing, I got the fuck out of there.

I peeled around the corner and knew the chase was on. Through my rearview I recognized the blue sedan from the other night, saw it weaving in and out of traffic and steadily gaining on me. A sanitation truck switched lanes and hugged Stepchild's tail, good, and a rattletrap station wagon blocked the other lane. The sedan tried to shimmy past the wagon, but the old geezer driving it wouldn't give an inch. Way to go, Pops.

The sedan dropped back behind the truck and leaned on its horn. In a heartbeat, I made a decision. I gripped the wheel, streaked across two lanes of traffic, narrowly missed the station wagon, and shot down a one-way street, ignoring the blare of horns that accompanied this move.

"Stepchild, don't fail me now." The car fishtailed, but I floored it and roared down the street as the Red Sea parted and cars moved out of my way. At the next intersection I jumped the light, and at Eighth Avenue I swung a left and bumped and bounced down the median strip until I could merge into traffic. A guy driving a Dodge next to me looked over, hesitated, and I zipped in front of him. He flipped me the bird, but that was the least of my worries.

I'd lost them. At least I hoped I had. I gulped air to calm my racked nerves and, mistake, inhaled the sour stench of my own body—the smell of fear. I was bathed head to toe in sweat. My shirt clung to me. I was shitting bricks and hoped to God they hadn't made the number on my license plate. Out of the frying pan and into the fire. I talked myself down until I could at last breathe normally.

It wasn't a good idea to return to the crib. No, I knew that. I looked over my shoulder at the duffel bag on the back seat. Had to get rid of it, no two ways about it. To throw it out the window was impractical. It'd start a riot—hell in Harlem for sure.

I drove aimlessly for the next half hour; then since it was close to noon, I parked, motor humming, and waited next to the front entrance of Columbia Hospital for Catherine to walk out.

I hadn't talked to her in days. Not since the night of Endless Love. She'd probably be surprised, pissed, and speechless, in that order, after I told her what was going on. She clammed up when she was angry. Okay, better give her the Disney version of the last few days.

She came out of the building, recognized the car, and hips rolling, glided toward me with that wonderful walk of hers. Some woman that was. I decided to be straight with her about the heroin before she stepped into the car. There went the Disney version.

I told her all of it. She looked at me as if she couldn't quite believe me. Who could blame her? She shook her head and directed me to drive to her apartment—lips pressed tight all the way. It was lunchtime, she said, and she had to fix her mother's lunch.

In her apartment, I gave her mother, Mrs. Walters, a quick greeting. The dope was tucked under my arm and I headed straight for the bathroom and locked the door. I found a razor in the cabinet over the sink, punctured the bags one by one, and dumped and flushed heroin for the next twenty minutes.

From outside the bathroom door I heard a knocking, and the very small Mrs. Walters inquired in a big foghorn voice, with West Indian directness, "My God, Catherine, what him doin' in dere, eh? You give he an enema?"

What else could I do? I grunted loud and long to reinforce her theory of things.

She padded away from the door and complained loudly, "God, him gone stink up the place to high heaven. Catherine, get the spray. What kind boyfriend you got?"

Catherine's response wasn't nice. She hollered back, loud enough so I could hear her, "The kind who's full of *shit*, Mama."

Okay, I stopped the grunts and instead serenaded both of them with a few bars of my old standby, "Nobody Knows de Trouble I've Seen"—which, in the present circumstances, was an honest expression of grief. I hesitated over the tags, then cut them off the bags and stuffed them into my pants pocket.

When I finally emerged from the bathroom I wandered through the large apartment and found Catherine in the kitchen, serving her mother lunch. Mrs. Walters glared at me over her soup, and said to Catherine, "Child, don't you be giving that boy nuttin' to eat."

What could I say? I smiled at Mrs. Walters.

"Hmph," she snorted. She wasn't impressed, dismissed me with a sour look, and returned to her bowl of soup. And that was that. Instant dislike. She hated me—I knew it.

I sighed. Another hill to climb. As I watched her eat, it occurred to me to ask a question that bubbled through my brain, "Do you happen to know Zeke Johnson, one of my tenants?"

She twitched her nose, and I saw a glimmer of something. "Zeke, him come from same island as me. Yes, works for me brother."

"Really?" I said, as if this were new information. "Doing what?"

I noticed Catherine, over her mother's shoulder, making furious signals at me behind her mother's back.

"Me brother buys and sells property. Makes plenty, plenty money. Zeke brings him good luck."

"Your brother sells property?"

"Um . . . yes, in real estate business."

I stared at her and at Catherine.

Catherine crossed her arms and amen-ed what her mother told me. "That's right, like Mama says, Uncle Harry's in *real estate*."

Did Catherine's mama live in dreamland? Was it possible that Harry's own sister didn't know how Harry made his living? I looked into Catherine's eyes and they affirmed what I suspected: her mother hadn't a clue. Unbelievable.

"Right, right, Mrs. Walters. Uh, about Zeke . . ."

Mrs. Walters ate soup while Catherine explained, "Zeke and my family are both from Trinidad." I nodded, and then she pointed across the room to what looked to be a small altar. Above it was a picture of the Virgin Mary and other assorted saints. "Courtesy of Zeke."

"What do you mean?" I was confused.

Catherine sighed. "As long as I can remember, Zeke has been a practicing bokor. A priest of sorts—of black magick—and a disciple of the Left Path. Many people, including Uncle Harry, and now my mother, believe in it."

I groaned inwardly. Zeke had told me about the Left Path and I hadn't known what he was talking about.

Mrs. Walters sucked her teeth at Catherine and cautioned, "Child, don't be bad-mouthing voodoo. A curse will rain down on you."

Catherine rolled her eyes and ignored her mother. She crossed to the altar and picked up a small sack embellished with sequins and feathers, similar to the one that sat on my desk—along with a multicolored glass necklace.

"Gris-gris," Catherine said. "This is supposed to protect my mother and destroy her enemies. This is the *job* Zeke does for Harry." She looked meaningfully at me. "Destroys his enemies."

I coughed. "I'm here to tell you Harry don't need no help," I said. It wasn't a secret the way Harry had made his bones. When he first got to New York, he took on two of the burliest heavy-duty gangsters around. About money they owed Harry. They wouldn't pay up and laughed at him. Harry laughed back and shot them stone dead right outside Biggie Small's club and walked away. Everybody tiptoed around Harry after that. They were still tipping, twenty years later. Me included. Harry was one crazy motherfucker.

Catherine's voice interrupted my thoughts. She said, "Zeke has Harry bamboozled as far as I'm concerned. Harry's used Zeke for years. And after my mother's heart attack, Zeke got her to believing." Catherine offered the bag.

I stared at the bag and turned it over in my hand. The power of belief. Mrs. Walters wasn't happy—she snatched it from me.

"Don't be messing with magick," she said.

I sat down at the kitchen table, across from Mrs. Walters. "Are you telling me Harry believes in voodoo?"

Mrs. Walters continued to eat, and Catherine stood behind her mother and gave her a squeeze. "Him and Mama. I've tried to talk her out of it. Won't work. Mama's become a believer, just like Uncle Harry. And it's not the good kind of voodoo, it's bad voodoo."

Mrs. Walters could hardly contain herself. She sputtered, and the vegetables she had ladled into her mouth shot across the table. Some of them landed on me. She declared, "Brought me back from death's door, you can't argue with that."

Catherine shook her head. "Good doctors and good medicine brought you back, Mama."

Mrs. Walters sucked her teeth and dabbed her napkin at soup trickling down her chin. "That's what *you* say. Her don' believe in the magick, but I know what's true."

Head deep in her soup she added, "Hear what I'm saying. Your mama be alive today if she'da used some of Zeke's magick."

Bull's-eye. Right between the eyes. I leaned across the table. "What do you know about my mother?" I said.

Mrs. Walters stopped her slurping. The whole room got quiet. Overhead, the fluorescent light hummed like dozens of bumblebees. She said carefully, "Everybody know her threw over Zeke to be with Montcrieff—everybody know that."

Catherine was caught off guard; I blinked in shocked surprise. I said slowly, "Not everyone."

Mrs. Walters raised her small head. "No?

I blinked again and responded, "No." And then, "What else do you know?"

"You play canasta?"

I eyed the old woman. "No," I said carefully.

"Good time to learn, don't you think? Catherine, get the cards and go back to school. Mr. Brown, him gone sit with this here old lady and play she some cards. Yes?"

She cast a sly eye at me. "Maybe I tell Mr. Brown some stories, eh?"

After Catherine left to go back to the hospital, I hunkered down to an afternoon of canasta. And Mrs. Walters didn't lie—she told me a whale of a story and advised me to put it in a pipe and smoke it. I did.

By late afternoon, I had learned the game and whupped Mrs. Walters's butt in canasta—many times and soundly. She didn't complain and seemed pleased as punch—so much so, she started calling me Amos. Go figure.

When she bedded down for her nap, I snuck out and headed for Brooklyn. Reba had some questions to answer, and I had discovered questions to ask.

Chapter 36

"Didn't I tell you to call before you came?" Reba said, as she swung the door wide to let me enter.

"Remember me, Reba? Hard head and a soft behind?"

A smile threatened at the edges of her frowning face. In fact, she seemed eager and excited. If I didn't know better, I'd have thought she was happy to see me.

This time she led me to her kitchen and sat me at the kitchen table while she poured iced tea into a large glass. It was a pleasant room, sunny and large, with herbs growing on top of every windowsill. I didn't wait; I slipped the sucker punch.

"You never told me my mother and Zeke were an item." If a nut-brown woman can turn white, then that's what Reba did. Her eyes blinked rapidly; I had caught her off guard.

"Where'd you hear that?" she demanded.

"Does it matter?"

She collapsed into the chair opposite me. "Guess not," she said.

"Want to tell me about it?"

Her face turned hard. "My sister was a silly girl and didn't know what she wanted."

"And what happened?"

"What do you mean? She changed her mind and married Montcrieff. That's all."

Reba's face shut like a trapdoor. The snap, sparkle, and vinegar fell away from the edges of her mouth and nostrils. I said, "Inform me, what the hell did my mother ever see in Zeke?"

She snapped, "If you were a woman, you'd know. He was handsome, had property, had money, and damn well knew how to spend it. In those days he was a catch."

"A lot of money to be made in chicken feathers?"

"What are you talking about?"

"The voodoo."

Reba reacted as if I had shot her. "You know about that?"

"Sure I know. He tried it out on me."

Reba recovered, crossed to the refrigerator, and began pulling food from it. "Black magick came later," she said. "After he got out of jail. After he lost his property. After he lost . . . everything."

"Why *black* magick?"

"Bitterness. Suited him. He'd always dabbled in it. He studied, became a bokor, and sold his services."

Services, I thought. For services rendered?

"What'd he do time for?"

She threw me a sharp look. "What do you think? Selling drugs. A black man's ticket to big money."

So that was the hookup to Harry, something more mercantile than the mere fact that they were countrymen. As Harry's personal sorcerer, Zeke had less mess, no stress. Like a parasite, he fed off of Harry. Zeke had secrets that he hadn't revealed.

Reba continued, "But he wasn't slick enough. Never slick enough—he was a fool." The slam of the refrigerator door punctuated her sentence. Reba was talking about something else now. I didn't comment; I let it ride.

And then I asked the question I had meant to ask Zeke—but in light of what I had found out from Mrs. Walters, seemed more important now.

"Which property did Zeke own?"

She hesitated a second before she spoke. "The one across the street from where you're living."

"The one where my mother was killed?"

"Yes."

So . . . Montcrieff wasn't the only one with a motive. I stared at her, my voice a whisper, and said, "You think Zeke killed my mother?"

Maybe she reacted to the intensity of my look. Maybe it was the harshness of my voice. She stuttered, "I—I ain't saying. All I know is Zeke was crazy jealous of everything your father had. Always taking from Montcrieff and pretending to be his friend."

"Well, Montcrieff did take his woman. Zeke had to be pissed. But why kill my mother? Why not kill the man—Montcrieff?"

Reba slammed a pot down on the stove. "Why you asking these questions now? It's forty years too late and won't do nobody a lick of good."

"Look, Reba, my mother was murdered. Strangled to death. Don't you think I deserve some straight answers?"

Reba gasped. "Strangled? My sister was strangled? Who told you that?"

I looked at her, puzzled by this outburst. "You didn't know that? Didn't the police tell you that?"

A whimper escaped from her throat. "No. Nobody told me nothing like that. They told me her neck was broken—they didn't say strangled. Lord Jesus."

"Reba," I said, "what difference does it make? That's how her neck got broken, by strangulation. Their forensic people could tell by the crushed bones in her neck."

At the last bit of news Reba got more agitated and slammed pots and banged pans around the kitchen, a whirlwind of activity. I couldn't be sure, but I thought tears glittered at the corners of her eyes. Had her sister's death all at once become real to her?

Silver threads of tears spilled down Reba's wrinkled cheeks—resignation and confusion fought for space inside her. "Some things . . ." she said, ". . . take a lifetime to learn." Then she turned back to a heartless stove and stirred the gravy that bubbled in a skillet.

"You're staying to supper." It wasn't a question; it was a statement. A terrible sadness cloaked Reba's form and bent her body farther, head facing the floor as she shuffled around the kitchen. Reba in pain was something wondrous to behold—something I had never seen, and I admit I was shocked. Did she mourn her sister, or her own life?

I relented. "Sure, Reba, I'll stay." She shot a grateful look my way. I buried the rest of my questions and stayed for dinner.

Chapter 37

After I left Reba, I drove around Brooklyn, taking stock of my situation and figuring out what the next step should be. Tall and Short were probably hot on my trail, and home, sweet home didn't seem like a good place to be right now.

I didn't pay attention to the gas gauge and drove myself right out of gas, and ended up stranded in a quiet Brooklyn neighborhood. From the fenced yards and all, it looked like I was deep in a white hood, and as far as I could tell, it was lights out for most of the people that lived there.

By my watch, it was only eleven o'clock. Still, not a good time to knock on white folks' doors, say I'm out of gas, can I use your phone? Big black men and nighttime create instant panic in white people. I didn't want to get shot, or worse, land in the pokey again.

So I spent the night in Hotel Stepchild, and squeezed my large frame into the back seat of the Cadillac and tried to stretch out. Tomorrow morning I'd look for a friendly face and borrow a gas can.

Sleeping in the car was rough going. I had to plant my feet up against the window, with my legs bent—which, of course, made my knees ache. Plus, the night was another muggy one, and my skin stuck to the seat. With each toss and turn, my skin went rip as I pulled sweaty arms, hands, and parts of my face off the seat like surgical tape.

Daybreak came before I knew it. I had just gotten to sleep when I felt a thump on the bottom of my feet. Somebody beat against the windows as if they were playing bongo drums. I snapped awake and looked out at one butt-ugly white man wearing Coke-bottle glasses with pockmarks the size of golf balls.

His pissant dog yipped like a nutcase at his side and scratched slivers of paint off Stepchild's doors with his paws. Motherfuck. I rolled the window down, shouted "Hey!" to the both of them, and leaped from the car like an attack dog.

Pockmarks was no fool—he wasn't looking to take me on. He cringed and pulled back five feet when he saw me coming and sputtered, "What was I doing in *his* neighborhood?" I told him the truth—I got lost and ran out of gas.

Even though daylight burned hot around us, the man was nervous in the service, you could tell. Still, he told me to hold on, and went off to his house; came back five minutes later with a can of gas. What do you know? A good Samaritan. In Brooklyn. I thanked him, said adios, and drove off.

Pockmarks watched me depart—huh, damn well made sure of it. I hoped like hell he hadn't taken down my license plate number.

I glanced at my watch—6:45 A.M. What does anyone do at 6:45 A.M.? At the nearest filling station I gassed up. Jesus, I thought, couldn't drive around all day. What to do? I found a coffee shop with a pay phone inside, dialed Seltzer, caught him at home, and came straight to the point.

"Anyone been looking for me?" I asked him.

"Love a parade?" he said.

I asked him for specifics and he laid it on me—city inspectors, Miss Ellie, Gloria, Wilbur, and oh yes, Harry's Blood Clots. The net was tightening.

I told him about my run-in with Short and Tall and instructed him to take a couple of days off, until I could find a way to remove those DEA bee stingers from my behind.

He asked me if I had a plan. I told him yeah, but not as good as the last one I had. Silence. Then a groan, and I told him I'd be in touch.

Seltzer said he'd make it a holiday, take his wife to the Bronx

Zoo. Why the zoo? I asked. I ragged that if his wife wanted to look at animals, she didn't have to go far, she had a bugger bear at home. He hung up on me. No sense of humor. My man Selz.

Since I was in a coffee shop, I ordered coffee and breakfast to go with it. I put a hurt on some melt-in-your-mouth waffles, ham slices, grits, eggs, and toast. And while I cogitated, smacking and snacking, my brain cells percolated.

Elizabeth and Zeke, I mused. Didn't seem possible. I couldn't fathom the two as a couple. What was my mother thinking?

And then I choked on my coffee as I had a god-awful thought. The waitress came to the table and slapped me on the back. She was a first-string linebacker type, so her slap brought tears to my eyes. I thanked her, paid the check, and split.

Reba. I had one final question to ask her. I didn't know if I was up to it, but the question had to be asked and answered. I was in Brooklyn anyway, so I had no excuse.

With me dressed in yesterday's rumpled clothes, Reba might wonder why I hadn't changed, but I didn't figure that to be important. While I drove I ruminated about Reba's reactions yesterday. She had surprised me. I frowned. Had age and circumstance softened Reba or had I been wrong about her all these years?

Sure, she had been hard on me when I was growing up, but had it been for my benefit? Had she been trying to protect me, after all? Reba was all I had of family, no matter what happened in the past. In her own way she offered a peace pipe. Was I big enough to accept it?

Twenty minutes later I pulled up on Reba's street. It was almost nine and hard to find a parking place. Down the street from her house I found a space, got out, was about to lock Stepchild's door when I got the shock of my life. A familiar figure thumped down the street, head down, cane in hand, coming toward me from the opposite direction.

Stunned, I watched him turn into Reba's walkway and up to her front door. He pulled out a key and entered. I made no attempt to hide myself, but he hadn't noticed, so focused was he on his destination.

I stood frozen, hand on the handle of Stepchild's door, while traffic whizzed past. I saw my future—a confused old man, standing in the middle of the street, bewildered, wondering who I was, where the hell I was going, and what the hell I was going to do.

In the end, I decided to find out what Zeke and Reba were up to and approached Reba's house. I bypassed the front, went through a side gate whose lock I easily opened, found the living room window, and peered through it. No luck. No one visible. I circled around the back of the house and trampled a rosebush planted next to the house, and then grappled for purchase on the ledge of a window that looked into the kitchen.

The scene looked domestic, the parties familiar as Reba moved about the kitchen, putting bundles of plants into a large grocery bag. Zeke sat and ate at the kitchen table, his moustache circling around and around as he chewed the breakfast laid in front of him.

I was confused. Yesterday Reba had made it clear that she suspected Zeke in her sister's murder—although now that I remember, she had done the same about Montcrieff. But here she was today, all cosy with Zeke. It didn't add up. But I could see that I had been a fool to entertain any idea of forgiveness with this woman. Reba couldn't be trusted—that was certain. What to do now, confront them?

I watched Reba reach into a cupboard and pull a bottle of rum, three-quarters full, off a shelf, tighten the cap, and then wrap newspapers around it and stuff it into a shopping bag. Then she shuffled toward the window where I was. I didn't budge. Belligerent, I wanted her to see me. I wanted her to know she had been caught at her game.

Startled at the vision of me in her window, she hesitated for only a second, then continued moving forward as if I weren't there. Her back toward Zeke, she picked the fresh herbs that grew in a box in the window while staring out at me and touched a finger to her lips. She wrapped the herbs carefully in more newspaper, and then she turned and shuffled back to Zeke. I didn't know what to think. I climbed down from my perch and returned to my car.

Sitting in the car I expelled a long breath and contemplated the situation and came up with more questions unanswered. What was Reba up to? I wanted to snatch Zeke by his collar and pummel him. It'd give me satisfaction, but it wouldn't give me proof of anything.

Maybe Reba had a better way. She was working on something, that was for sure, and she obviously knew things that I didn't. Leave it to her? Okay—for now. I had plenty else to take care of. I turned over Stepchild's engine. If Reba came up with something tangible to cook Zeke's goose, I'd turn it over to Bundt. Get him working on it.

I had to get back to my place. The guns were there and it was looking like I'd have to use them. Best to return home under the cover of night. Where to go until then? The zoo? And then I thought, Canasta anyone?

Mom Walters—that's what she had wanted me to call her when I left her yesterday afternoon—was tickled pink when I drove up.

I took a shower at her place, made a few calls, confirmed that I could catch Steadwell later that evening, and Mrs. Walters—Mom—broke out a bottle of sherry. We raided the refrigerator and I threw together some leftovers. She called Catherine to let her know she had a date for lunch, and not to bother coming home. After that we settled in for a long afternoon of cards. Whipped her ass again. She loved it.

I left Mrs. Walters at dusk, missed Catherine on purpose, and headed over to see Steadwell, who lived in an apartment off St. Nicholas and 140th Street, keeping one eye peeled for the dark blue sedan or the Clots' Cadillacs.

Chapter 38

"What I want to know is, what made you think you could get away with something like that with Harry? Boy, thought you had better sense than to be messing with some dope." Steadwell paced the floor of his small studio apartment, puffing on a cigarette and stinking up the place. In the fifteen minutes I had been there, he had consumed four cigarettes, and a haze hung from the ceiling like a fog. It was his apartment, so what could I say?

"What's done is done, Steadwell."

Steadwell pushed six mink coats off a chair onto the floor and sat. "Every day somebody be dying over that shit. You hear about Skidmore?"

"No, what?"

"OD'd off some smack. They found him in the street yesterday, body stiffer than a thirteen-year-old's dick. Dead. That stuff ain't nothing but poison."

"Yeah, I know, that's why I dumped it down the toilet." We both got quiet. Then the idea hit me like a thunderbolt, and I sat straight up. "Yeah, poison, *that's* why I got rid of it—the stuff was no good. That's it, Steadwell."

Steadwell eyed me, disbelief cresting like waves over his face. "Are you facking or cracking? You for real?"

A plan unfolded. I was getting excited now. "Facts, man. Don't you see? That dope killed poor Skidmore, and who knows? Maybe a few others. Yes, it was that dope that killed him. So I had to get rid of it before anybody else got their hands on it."

Steadwell shook his head and sighed. "Harry ain't stupid, Amos. Only way he'll listen to that hogwash is if you get his money back and serve up those two agents."

"Well, that's what I'll have to do, won't I?" I thought for a minute. "Put it out on the street, Steadwell, would you? That I'm gunning for those two agents."

"Why don't you tell Harry directly?"

"Uh, like you said, cash in hand makes Harry a better listener. Anyway, chances are he'll believe the grapevine before he'd believe me."

"You got a point. Okay, I'll spread the word. Messing with my rep if somebody finds out, but I'll spread the word. You got a plan?"

Why did everyone keep asking that? "Sure," I muttered and headed for the door. Then I paused and said, "And what about the other? What we were talking about?"

Steadwell looked down at the floor. "You ain't heard nothing from me. I don't know nothing about nothing, hear? But between you and me and the gatepost, take a long hard look in the mirror—tell you everything you need to know."

Hand on the doorknob, I locked eyes with Steadwell. "Yeah, okay, right. Check you later, Steadwell."

He ground his cigarette butt in an ashtray and shook his head again. His sigh blew through the room. "Hope there's going to be a later, Amos."

I looked at him and down at the crushed cigarette. I hoped so too.

For what I needed to do next I had to get some help and headed up to the Bronx, to Seltzer's pad. The ghetto's creed was about to come into play—do unto others before they do it to you. Those two DEA agents were stuck in my crosshairs and heavy on my mind.

Seltzer lived in a concrete jungle of a housing complex with over five hundred families in it, its exterior dark, depressing, and shabby and not too welcoming. I made it past the outdoor buzzer, past a security guard, up a crappy elevator, before ringing the doorbell to

Seltzer's apartment. Susie, Seltzer's dog, jumped up to greet me, two paws deep into my chest. Seltzer's wife, Delphina, sat on a couch, shredding wet tissues between her fingers and sobbing.

When she paused between sobs I found out I arrived too late—that after I had talked to Seltzer this morning, somebody had jumped him. He had stepped outside his apartment to dump the garbage and when he hadn't returned after twenty minutes, Delphina said she went down the hall to look and found him, lying unconscious, near the trash disposal, bleeding buckets—his blood splattered against the walls and floor of the hallway. She called for an ambulance—nobody had witnessed the beating—and had sat with Seltzer all day at Einstein Hospital, his condition critical.

I had caught her just as she was about to take off for the hospital again with a bag of personal items to take to Seltzer. She'd only just returned home, to feed the dog, she said, and make dinner for her teenage grandson.

In the middle of her pain, she stopped and inquired about me. "I'm sorry about your mother, Amos. James told me what happened. Must have been an awful shock."

Well, you can guess how I felt. "That's . . . that's ancient history. It's you and Seltzer I'm worried about. Did you see anything at all? Did Seltzer say who did it?"

"Security downstairs says two white guys came looking for Seltzer. They flashed badges, so he let them in. I don't know why they'd be looking for Seltzer. He ain't done nothing, I'd swear on it. They didn't come in—caught him in the hallway. Seltzer came to for a while this morning, but he didn't say nothing. Couldn't—hard for him to talk, face all busted up, teeth knocked out. I let him rest. Nurse give him something for the pain and he go out cold again."

It was hard to hear this. The muscles in my jaw tensed, then softened at the sight of Delphina. She looked pretty worn herself. Dark shadows circled her eyes, and her bosom heaved with emotion. I tried to comfort her. "Listen, I'll take Seltzer's things to him and sit with him the rest of the evening. You get some rest and look after your grandson. Visit Seltzer in the morning—he ain't going nowhere."

She thought about it and said, "Sure you right," grateful to be relieved, adding, "Don't want to leave Clarence here by himself. Who knows what might happen? And you know the hospital won't allow the boy to visit up on James's floor."

I nodded, gathered Seltzer's belongings, and said good-bye to Delphina—revenge and mayhem on my mind. I had to get to the guns. Sons of bitches weren't going to get away with this. Something had to be done, and I was going to do it.

Chapter 39

Seltzer was wrapped tighter than a mummy in his hospital bed. Only his eyes and forehead showed between the wrappings of bandages. Short and Tall had done a number on him. His jaw, nose, and leg had been broken. They were making sure I got the message. Well, I knew who I was dealing with. Trouble is, the fools didn't know who *they* were dealing with.

The thing about trouble . . . having it creates the capacity to handle it—read that somewhere. They were going to regret the day they met up with me, for sure.

Caww—hiccup. Caww—hiccup. The noise of the oxygen machine cut through the silence in the room. The time was nearly midnight. I got up to leave and leaned next to Seltzer's ear and told him, "They ain't getting away with it, old buddy, don't you worry." I smashed my hat down on my head and the oxygen sighed as I left the room.

No one in sight. I cut across the Assembly of God's rear lot at the end of my block and squeezed through a slat in a broken fence. My shirt caught a nail and ripped like a fart through the Harlem night. I waited. No barking dog responded. And no light in the vicinity told on me.

I stood in darkness beneath the fire-escape ladder that hung from the building next to the church. Higher than I thought. It took me four leaps before I finally hooked on to the ladder. I kicked my legs back and forth as I tried to hoist myself up. It had been years since I tried this stunt, but I didn't remember that scaling a fire escape had been this hard back when I was a kid. Shit, and back then I was a hell of a lot shorter too. I couldn't understand it. My hat flew off as I pulled my bulky body up the ladder. God, I hoped none of the neighbors would catch me.

Through an open window on the second story, I saw the glow of a black-light poster and heard Barry White's bass rumble out of a stereo speaker inside, while a woman did a slow grind with herself and got a nut.

I heard a moan and . . . , "Sing it, Barry, awww, sukey, sukey now," as I trod as soft as I could past her window on the way to the roof. Not quiet enough. My foot scraped the railing. From inside her apartment I heard her shout, "Hey," and I froze.

"Hey," she said again.

The stereo's volume lowered. She stuck her head out the window and looked down into the dark yard, head turning to the right and left. Quiet, she listened for another moment and muttered, "Huh."

Visions of me being arrested again, this time as a Peeping Tom, motored through my mind as I waited—and she waited. Satisfied at last that there was no one in the yard, she pulled her head back in and returned to Barry and amphed her stereo up to the max. Barry didn't miss a stroke, no, sir. He moaned and sang, "I've got so much to give. . . ."

Thank you, Barry.

I climbed higher up. The ladder creaked and swayed under my weight. Good thing Barry was busy. Everyone's window was wide open. Televisions blared inside the toaster-oven apartments, but hardly anyone sat watching. Most people had camped out front on stoops and chairs, to escape the stifling July heat.

When I reached the top I held on to the roof's ledge and pulled myself up and over. I didn't stand to my full height for fear of being seen from below, so I monkey-walked to the front of the building and peered over the side.

The card games were in session, the street as lively at night as it was in the daytime. Nobody slept. Seventies unemployment and humidity kept people up way past their bedtimes.

Uh-oh. I drew back from the edge. Couldn't be sure, but was that Short and Tall's blue sedan parked halfway down the block? Couldn't tell. In this light and at this distance it could be blue, black, or brown.

They'd bring attention to themselves if they parked too long on the street. Unless, of course, they didn't care. That was a possibility. I squinted my eyes, still couldn't tell for sure. Did they do like I did—park a few blocks over? Were they standing in the overhang of one of these buildings, waiting? My jaw tensed, the anger returned.

Two things I needed to do, get the guns and have a talk with Zeke, and to do that I needed to get inside my building. Ape-style, I made my way across dozens of rooftops, recalling the fun I used to have as a child. For a fleeting moment I forgot the present danger and ran free. Running the roofs and eluding the cops. The more things change, the more they stay the same.

A roof is to hide. A roof is halfway to the sky. A roof is to dream. A roof is . . . a place to smoke dope. I saw them before they saw me. Two stoned kids. I hollered at them and they scurried off the roof. Fucking juvenile delinquents, what'd they think they were doing? Never mind that I did the same thing when I was a kid.

When I reached my building, I did a reverse. I climbed down the fire escape and tapped on the window of the top floor—Wilbur's apartment. His window was open, but the shades were drawn. Hair in rollers, he peered around the shades real casual-like, as if discovering me outside on the fire escape was no big thing.

"Mr. B.?"

"Wilbur," I whispered, "can you let me in?"

"Sure, sugar. Um . . . I wasn't expecting company. Let me put on a robe."

"Fuck the robe, Wilbur, I'm coming in, pull the shade up."

"Aren't we in a snit?" he said. With a grand gesture, he snapped the window shade and it rolled to the sky. And so did his dick. Jesus. I didn't know the cat was buck naked. I guess I blushed and kept my eyes glued pretty much to the floor as I climbed through his window.

"Put your damn robe on, Wilbur."

He complied, then the little pussy puckered his lips. I shook off the gesture like a dog shakes water. He noticed and let me have it.

"There's a nerve running through this room. A big black one. Invading my privacy, and got the nerve to—"

Okay, okay, I admit it—it was the gay part. It still bothered me. "Sorry, Wilbur."

He pursed his lips together again and adjusted a hair roller. "Say it like you mean it."

I gave him a don't-you-fuck-with-me look, and he backed off.

"All right, I forgive you," he said quickly. "People been looking for you."

"How did you know?"

"How could I not know? Two men came calling twice. Nobody here in the daytime except me, so I answered the door. They flashed some badges and gave me grief. The last time, the assholes pushed me up against the mailboxes, but I didn't tell 'em shit. Course I don't know shit, but they didn't know that. They wanted to know where you were."

Why did Wilbur always make me feel guilty? Awkwardly, I thumped him on the arm. "Thanks, Wilbur. I mean it, man. I'll take care of them. May be gone for a while. Keep a lookout around here for me." I headed for the door.

"Oh, Mr. B., about Patty . . ." Wilbur said.

I turned.

He saw my look and said, "Uh, never mind . . ."

I waited. When Wilbur didn't offer any more I said, "She's into that shit again, ain't she?"

Wilbur nodded yes.

I flashed back to when the cops had pulled me screaming and kicking out of Reba's house. I resisted with everything I had, but when they shoved me into the back seat of the police car, it was over. I lost hope. When Wilbur nodded yes about Patty, that same feeling took over and rocked me hard where I stood.

"Is she home?"

"Ain't been home for a couple of days. Josie's sleeping at Winnie's. I ain't got room here, but I take care of Josie in the daytime."

Wasn't anything I could do but nod. I left Wilbur's room, noticed a light on under Zeke's door, hesitated, then tapped lightly. No answer. I put my ear to the door. Silence inside. I licked my lips. No matter. I wasn't quite ready to talk to him anyway. I left and trod quietly down the stairwell—didn't want the other tenants to know I was in the building.

When I reached the foot of the stairs, I froze. The bulb was out in the entryway. Senses alert, I moved cautiously through the darkened hallway. Too late I felt air whiz past me and felt something hard crack against my skull. Tweet-tweet and lights out as I fell, unconscious, to the floor.

Chapter 40

Ever had your head hurt so bad that when you blinked your eyes you couldn't stand the pain? That was what it was like when I finally came to, sprawled across the sofa in my living room. Sitting opposite me was The Beast with Five Fingers, Harry's Blood Clot George, asleep in a chair, gun dangling off the end of one of his pudgy fingers. I shifted to a sitting position while I watched the room kaleidoscope and heard Big Ben clang like a motherfucker inside my head.

Should I snatch George's gun? Even the effort to think exhausted me, so I knew I was in no shape to snatch anybody's gun away. I fell back on the sofa's cushion, my head throbbing in counterpoint to the thudding of my heart.

The move awakened George, who opened one Cyclop eye and glared at me out of it.

"Where the fuck you been?" he said. "Where the dope? Where the money?"

Holding my head in my hands, I rolled my eyeballs, ever so carefully, to survey the room. Trashed—my décor gone to shit. I turned my head—ouch—to look beyond the room. Ditto the rest of my apartment. George hadn't found what he was looking for. Nor would he.

"What'd you have to hit me in the head for, George? That wasn't necessary."

George looked at me blankly, shrugged his shoulders, and repeated, "Where the dope, where the money?"

A lightbulb came on. George didn't know shit from Shinola about what happened to the heroin, or the money. That's why his ass was here, playing wrecking ball in my apartment. He was knocked out flatter than a pancake when Short and Tall took the money and split. Yeah, but why didn't Zeke tell him what went down? I pondered that and kept my lip zipped. When in doubt, shut your mouth—a saying I picked up in the joint, and it's served me well over the years. I said nothing and stared back at George. Made him crazy. He jumped to his feet and waggled his gun at me.

"Give it up," he screamed, "or me blow your head off."

"Ain't got it, George, none of it," I said. "If you wanted to blow my head off, you would have done it way before now, so let's get to why you're really here. Let me guess. Harry's in your ass. He's blaming you for all of it. Am I right?"

His lips trembled like Jello-O. His eyes turned a fiery red. Bingo.

"Well, man, what can I say? The truth is, you didn't protect Harry's interests. Neither did Zeke." I sneaked a peek from beneath my eyebrows, shook my head, and double tsked for his benefit. "You let Harry down. Let those DEA guys get away with the skag *and* the money? That's deep, George."

His face fell and puddled on top of his chest. The man was scared. Great. Maybe a way to pull myself out of this after all.

"You explain to Harry—you tell him how it was," he said.

"Hey, ain't my job, man, and you know Harry, he don't want to hear no excuses. Besides, ain't you a little bit embarrassed? There were four of us and only two of them."

Fireworks popped behind George's eyes. I knew that would get to him. I noticed George's clothes—same suit he had on the night of the drug buy.

He said, "Told me come get you."

That was a fat lie. George wanted a scapegoat for Harry's wrath. He was ducking Harry too—I could tell from his clothes. "Well, George, Harry's gonna have to wait."

George pointed his gun at me. "Now," he commanded.

I wasn't threatened. I held the trump card and George knew it. I talked real slow and explained to him that those DEA guys had Harry's money and we had to get it back. The heroin was no good—they had tried to scam Harry.

"Got to find those guys, understand? They're in with Narcotics out of the Twenty-eighth Precinct, working for the DEA. You know who the DEA is, right?" George nodded. His lower jaw hung down. "After we get the money back, *then* we go see Harry. Harry wouldn't be too happy to see us now. No dope. No money."

"No dope? No money?" George asked, and looked down at the floor. He was thinking.

I didn't want him to hurt himself, so I said, "Need some backup, George, think you can arrange that? Then we go see Harry. If we get the money back, Harry will think you're a hero."

The idea simmered in George's head, about five minutes. I waited. Then he grunted twice and headed for the door. "Two hours. Be back with some boys in two hours."

Thank God for stupid people. After George left I jumped to my feet, and what did I do that for? Nausea lurched through my gut and up into my throat. What in the hell did George have to hit me for? I willed the nausea away while I felt for the bump—the size of a small lemon—in the back of my head. Didn't matter—I didn't have time for pain. I had to work fast.

I hurried out of my apartment and into my office and headed straight for Montcrieff's file cabinet. I whipped through the pile of loose pictures and rescued the pictures I wanted. One of Reba, in between Montcrieff and Zeke, arms draped around their shoulders. Another of Montcrieff and Elizabeth in a park, having a picnic. The last picture, all four of them in happier times, dressed in Sunday go-to-meeting clothes, Zeke, Reba, Montcrieff, and Elizabeth. And yes, the picture of Reba and Zeke. I stuffed them in my shirt pocket, grabbed the master keys, and climbed up the stairs to the top floor.

I banged on Zeke's door this time, and Wilbur popped his head out of his apartment and told me, "He ain't there. Ain't seen him in a couple of days."

"The light's on. It was on last night." I used the keys and tried to open Zeke's door. Five minutes into it I realized Zeke must have changed the locks—the key didn't work. Wilbur, propped against the door, watched me struggle for a couple of minutes, then disappeared into his apartment. He came out with a fingernail file, fiddled with the lock, and it clicked open.

I rolled my eyes but resisted comment and entered Zeke's studio apartment. Wilbur peered over my shoulder as I halted just inside the door. A potpourri of odors assaulted my nostrils. Uneaten soup sat in a flowered bowl on top of Zeke's kitchen table, beside it a shot glass and a bottle of rum that I recognized.

The tools of Zeke's mystical trade lay in piles all over the place—pots of crushed herbs and powders, bunches of flowers and weeds, feathers, chicken feet, strings, ropes and ribbons and other strange stuff I couldn't identify. Dozens upon dozens of small bags lay about, waiting to be filled, with black magick potions. Well, that, I thought, wasn't going to happen any time soon.

There lay Zeke, face up in his bed, eyes staring and obviously dead.

Chapter 41

I approached Zeke's body—his form stiff and unmoving. I stared down at him. I couldn't begin to explain what I felt at that moment. And then I got the shock of my life. Zeke's eyes blinked. I jumped back. The man looked like a corpse, but he was still breathing, his breath shallow and slow. His skin was clammy when I felt for a pulse, his body rigid. His eyes followed my movements. A sheen of perspiration coated his face.

"Wilbur, call an ambulance, he's alive."

Wilbur moved with lightning speed to the phone. No questions asked—there wasn't time and he knew it.

Zeke's face looked like a death mask, his eyes yellow. I leaned in to Zeke and said, "Hang on, Zeke, help is coming." He looked at me with an expression I hoped never to see again.

"Mine," he said. Spittle oozed from his lips. Then he said it again, more forcefully. "Mine."

"What's yours, Zeke? What?" I searched his face. "The brownstone, is that what you're talking about? The brownstone belongs to you?"

He smiled at me. Can you believe it? The vengeful bastard smiled at me. I knew he was dying, but I couldn't stay quiet. I whispered close to his ear, "I know about you and my mother."

He smiled that horrible smile again, his lips trembled, and with great effort he gripped my shirt and pulled himself nearer. His fingers were icy cold. “Mine. Your father—your father . . .”

“What is it, Zeke? Say it.”

His eyes glittered, his face contorted. He spat out, “Nigger Landlord.”

I had nothing to say to him. He fell back on the bed. And then he died. Simple as sin. No angels chorused above. No one wept below. He just died. Zeke was dead—his son by his side.

Chapter 42

I called the city morgue, and they called the police, so technically it wasn't my doing that got Bundt and Caporelli involved again, so I couldn't understand what Bundt's harangue was about.

"Don't believe in coincidences, Brown. Two victims in two months? How'd you get that tear on your shirt? You've got some explaining to do," Bundt said.

The police had been in the building over three hours. According to Winnie and some of the neighbors, two carloads of thugs were parked directly down the block and police cars whizzed past them, not noticing a thing.

And Wilbur buzzed in my ear that the guys that roughed him up were slouched down in a blue sedan at the opposite end of the block. How's that for coincidence?

Cops tramped up the stairs to the third floor and back down again. I watched the parade through the open door of my office and saw when Zeke's body bag bounced down the stairs on a stretcher. It could have been a sack of potatoes the way they handled the body.

No activity on the street, except for the police cars coming and going. Kids were locked up in their homes tighter than presents at Christmas—the street quiet. And these cops standing next to me, asking me a hundred questions, had no clue.

I brought my attention back to Bundt's questions and inspected the rip in my shirt. "What would you like me to explain? This? I tore it on a nail sticking out of a fence." The truth was easy.

The two detectives eyeballed me with poker faces.

"Oh, come on," I added. "You don't seriously think I had anything to do with the old man's death? He was alive when me and Wilbur found him. What? I went up there, said boo to him, he had a heart attack?"

Caporelli put his two cents in. "Wasn't his heart, wiseass. It was murder, plain and simple. Poisons all over the place. Did you know rhododendrons are poisonous?"

I stared at him.

Caporelli shrugged. "A *Jeopardy* question—the category was poisonous flowers."

"Caporelli, button it," Bundt said.

"Maybe it was suicide," I said.

"Maybe not. Can you think of any reason he might have killed himself? Definitely a suspicious death."

I shrugged my shoulders. "No."

Bundt stepped toward me and rumbled in my ear, "Listen, Brown, you got something you ain't telling me?"

I looked him square in his face. "I got a lot I ain't telling you, 'cause if I remember rightly, you don't want to know. Maybe Zeke's death is *drug-related*. You want to try that on for size?"

That brought Bundt up short and he shot a glance at his partner. "What are you talking about?" he said.

"Tried to give you heads-up on that, but you didn't listen. DEA. And news flash—some person or *persons* in your precious Twenty-eighth Precinct, Narc Unit, is probably involved."

The muscles bunched in Bundt's jaw and he told Caporelli to shut the office door.

"What the fuck's he talking about, Hal?" Caporelli said softly.

"I ain't got a clue. What the hell are you talking about, Brown?"

And then I laid it out, like a corpse at his feet.

I wasn't crazy, stupid neither. Those cats were in bed with somebody out of that precinct, I'd bet my watch. From what I had pieced together I figured Short and Tall worked with somebody dirty at the Twenty-eighth, and who knows? Maybe other precincts as well. The feds had a leaky storage tank too. The kilos I had been given had evidentiary tags, so it was "misplaced" heroin coming from evidence storage and somebody on the inside on the take.

Since Tall had so generously promised to provide heroin on a continuous basis, he was receiving it on a continuous basis, had to be, and that told me he had to have some stashed somewhere, waiting to move it.

If drug dealers like Harry could be believed, and I, for one, believed him on this, the alphabet agencies were involved up to their eyeballs. Complicit, I think the word is. Drugs poured into this country like rain, and wasted whole populations of black people in big cities everywhere. Like Patty. Made me sick to my stomach to think about it. Well, somebody had to stand up to this carnage.

"Cherchez the drugs, man, and check your own house. This could be a promotion for you. Bet somebody in your department would like to see this drain plugged. Aren't there any honest cops around?"

Bundt turned a rosy red and asked me, "Where'd you get your information?"

"I live in Harlem, man. I don't have to look for nothing; it comes to me. Two white men knocked on my door yesterday." I quickly described Short and Tall and identified them as the same pair I had run into at the Twenty-eighth Precinct.

And then I said, "The old man upstairs, he worked for Harry Algonquin Bridges—heard of him? You put two and two together and you're bound to come up with four." Or six or five or eight, but I wasn't telling them that. Disinformation, I think that's the term. And what's a little misdirection between friends? And a little heat on Harry couldn't be a bad thing.

I pulled tags from my pocket and threw them down one by one on the desk. DEA, four. NYPD, six. NYPD was ahead by two.

"Where'd you get these?" Caporelli said and he reached for them. I looked across at Bundt.

Bundt snatched the tags out of Caporelli's hands and inspected them. Let Caporelli play catch-up—it wasn't my concern.

"Ain't you at least angry, man?" I pointed upstairs. "I mean, the DEA's making more work for you. A homicide—that's your job, ain't it? Investigating homicides?" Bundt caught my drift.

"Let's go," he said and pushed a bewildered Caporelli out of the room. At the door he turned. "I'll see what I can do. Can't promise anything. Only what I'm *able* to do, understand? You still ain't out of the woodpile. Make no mistake, Brown, we'll be back."

Nigger in the woodpile, huh? I watched them leave. In fact, I watched as their car zoomed right by the blue sedan at the end of the block.

Make no mistake, the man said. I heard him. Good advice.

The tenants packed into my office—all of them. Except for Patty. She was nowhere to be found. Wilbur had Josephine hanging off his hip. The new tenant, Oscar, looked like he was about to wet his pants. Winnie sat on a folding chair, the only one in the room crying over Zeke's demise. They asked a million questions. You could tell they were scared.

Everybody knew something was about to go down. Not a soul stirred on the street outside. The mugginess was intense, the sky dark and threatening. The neighbors were anxious and my phone rang off the hook. Even the pastor down the street called, wanted to know what to tell his flock. I told him to get the flock out of there.

I reassured everybody as much as I could and pledged to do something. After all, this was my doing. I didn't let the other neighbors in on it, but I had to come clean with my tenants, and it was hard. I took the receiver off the hook and laid it on the desk.

"It's about drugs."

Still weeping, Winnie said, "Everything in Harlem is about drugs, everything, and I'm sick to death of it." The others murmured their agreement.

"Frieda-down-the-block's two children done gone to drugs. Charlotte Ferguson's son is dead, and Patty—Lord help her, what's happened to her?"

"That ain't the half of it, Winnie. What about the ones in jail—in hospitals?" said Wilbur.

"I know, I know. I see what's going on same as you. I don't want to see it neither. Hard times and funny money. But what's happening today, I got to let you know, it's my fault."

"How's it your fault, Mr. B.? You the only somebody around here trying to do something about the drugs," Wilbur said.

Straight up I said, "Yeah, well, I did something I ain't proud of, and it's biting my ass." Nobody spoke—I could guess what they thought. "You have my word, I'm getting the drug dealers off the block."

"But, Mr. B., you only one man. How you going to—"

"Nobody on this block gets hurt. These people are after me. I'm going to take my car and lead Harry's men and the blue sedan out of this neighborhood. Unfortunately, it'd ruin my plans if I got shot before I got to my car, so I'm going to need help with a disguise."

Oscar and Winnie looked blank. Wilbur was the first to speak. "Anything, Mr. B. You got it. We're behind you."

So what if Wilbur was light in the loafers? The man was righteous. I looked at him and swore to myself I'd never think another bad thought about him. That promise didn't last. I had another bad thought. But what happened was, it triggered an idea and I turned to Winnie. "Winnie, lend me your dress."

Both Wilbur and Oscar looked surprised, but I was beyond caring. Winnie caught on quick and bustled into action. She pounded upstairs, and a few minutes later her dress sailed over the railing. "You need shoes? A purse?" she shouted.

"Your shoes won't fit me, Winnie."

"Sandals, Mr. B., that'll work," said Wilbur. He was getting excited.

In ten minutes, I was dressed and ready to go. I would have made any transvestite proud. Wilbur beamed. He wanted to put makeup on me, but I resisted and told him not to get carried away. A breeze whizzed past my crotch, so I put my pants back on and rolled the cuffs up so they wouldn't show beneath the dress. Wilbur said it destroyed the "line," but I ignored him. Then I asked Winnie to empty her purse and give it to me. I put the three guns and some rounds in it. Everyone got hysterical, but I assured them I'd only use it to protect myself.

I asked Oscar to take care of everybody while I was gone. Wilbur got huffy and said, "Oh, puh-lease," as if his manhood was insulted. Think I could figure that one out? Everybody wished me luck.

I looked neither to the right nor to the left as I clumped down the brownstone steps, crossed the street, and headed to where Stepchild was parked, only about twenty yards from the blue sedan.

Mine was the only movement on the block. As I walked, a dark cloud passed overhead. Superstitious? Not me.

The sky crackled a warning, then rumbled, low and ominous. Who should appear but Big Butt, drunk as a skunk, weaving down the block and fucking waving to me.

"Nigger Landlord," she shouted and started humping toward me. So much for disguises.

I beat it to my car. Big Butt was closing ground. At the other end of the block a car engine started. "Get away, get away before you get hurt," I screamed.

Lightning split the sky. Big Butt hesitated and looked up, confused. I jumped into the car and Stepchild leaped into action. I gunned her motor, pulled off Winnie's wig, and tossed it to Short and Tall as I sped past them.

They hooked a U and came after me. No sooner had they spun around than I jammed on the brakes, shifted into reverse, streaked backward past them, then jerked the wheel and did a hard U of my own. I heard the screeching of brakes and the sedan whipped around again.

Waiting at the other corner were the Clots. I tore past them as well. Relief poured through me. Both cars were on my tail. At least I got them out of this hood and off the block.

Traffic was heavy. The bicentennial, July 4, was tomorrow and celebrants were already in the streets. I weaved in and out of pedestrians and cars and headed to the Bronx, a strange caravan behind me.

The heavens had opened, and rain beat against my windshield. Still people streamed in the downpour over to the Hudson River to watch the festivities and see thousands of tall ships and other small boats sail up and down. Audiences crowded along the shoreline to hear the bands and see the entertainment. I made slow progress, but my trackers were still behind me.

The highway was closed to traffic, so I kept to city streets. Something happening at Yankee Stadium too. I traveled past the stadium and headed for what I remembered was an isolated area and open spaces beyond the warehouses off the Hudson, the cars still trailing. My heart was thumping. A good place for a showdown.

Chapter 43

As soon as we hit wide-open spaces, Short and Tall wised up to the Clots on their tail and tried some evasive moves. Behind me I heard shots—the blue sedan peeled suddenly off to the left. The Clots followed. The sedan sped toward the bank of warehouses, and the chase began for real.

I swung Stepchild's wheel in their direction, ground the accelerator into the floor until Stepchild's frame shook in protest, the speedometer's needle shivering at a hundred miles an hour. Ahead, the sedan turned left and I watched as it burned rubber and raced down a cobbled alley, the Clots' cars not far behind.

I sped past the alley's entrance and rushed ahead to the next one. The burp of a machine gun repeated in the distance. Jesus. I geared Stepchild down, hung a left, and shocks catching hell, bounced down a cobbled alley to cut off the blue sedan.

Menlo's Meatpacking Warehouse loomed into view at the far end of the alley in a cul-de-sac. Just as I figured, the blue sedan appeared and skidded around the cul of the sac and headed straight for me.

I stomped on my brakes, and Stepchild fishtailed to the right and came to rest across the width of the alley. I yanked on the hand brake, grabbed Winnie's purse, and hauled ass out of the car. Shit, the dress I wore wrapped itself around my pant legs, and I stumbled to the ground. The sedan's brakes howled. I scrambled up, but the sedan kept coming.

Perfume misted in vapors from the dress as the odor mingled with the heat of my body. I jumped out of the sedan's path just in time and pressed myself against a brick wall of the nearest building and hung on for dear life as the car plowed sideways into Stepchild. Wham. Damn. Thank you, ma'am. Stepchild skidded like an eight ball spinning toward a corner pocket. Sound filled the narrow alley. More brakes screamed bloody murder. Before the Clots' cars hit, doors flew open and a dozen bodies hurtled through the air.

Have you evah seen an elephant fly-y-y?

It was surreal. Visions of Meat Mouth, a young punk, back from the Vietnam War, Eighty-second Airborne, gone all nutty two months before. Nigger jumped off the top of a tenement building, arms spread like an eagle, singing that song from that Disney *Dumbo* flick, his body plunging to the pavement. It was just like that.

The sound from the crunching metal roared in my ears. Hell, I wasn't no fool—I stayed plastered to the wall and hung by my fingernails.

The next chain of events left me stupid. Harry's ghetto army leaped into action, professionals at work. Harry always bragged about his "army" and here was a bona fide demonstration, a paramilitary maneuver happening before my eyes—Harry's homeboys, armed and dangerous. They fell on Short and Tall like maggots on meat.

I shouted, "Hold it," hiked up the dress, and sprinted toward the men who were dragging Short and Tall out of the smoking wreckage.

George the Blood Clot cussed up a blue streak in the middle of the alley, a gun in one hand and a handkerchief stuffed into the wideness of his bleeding nostril. He bellowed to his men to bring Short and Tall to him. Pinned behind the wheel of the crumpled sedan, barely conscious, Tall was dragged out last and dumped, like rubbish, to the ground.

Short lay in the street and screamed like a banshee. He clutched his left leg with one hand and clawed the ground with the other. George, with his sensitive self, kicked the man's broken leg, then jammed his gun into Short's ear, ready to waste him when I shouted,

"*George*, the point is to get back the money. How we going to do that if he's dead?"

George froze. The wheels ground slowly in his head and I smelled the smoke. "If they're dead, how's that gonna happen, huh?" I repeated.

Short looked up at me and snarled, "You double-crossing son of a bitching . . ." He took in my attire and screamed, ". . . Faggot!"

Payback time. Now I knew how Wilbur felt—a painful moment. I looked down at the man, sanding his nails on the cobbled bricks, and said, "Never mind, George, shoot the bastard."

Short screamed.

"Sticks and stones, motherfucker, ain't gonna get you nowhere. Harry ain't doing business with you no more," I said.

Where'd that come from? Was I entitled to speak for Harry? Hell, Harry dubbed me a duke, who better? The bottom line, Harry wasn't there to argue.

And then I bent down and drawled in his ear, "Your shit was poison, see? Harry wants his money back."

George stood nearby, agitated. George didn't like secrets, so I said loudly, "That's right. Harry wants his money back. If I was you, man, I'd cooperate and tell George here everything he wants to know, and I'd end each and every sentence with a *please*, *thank-you*, or *sir*."

George smiled at that. Everyone likes a little respect. With dead eyes, George shot a round into the brick next to Short's pinkie finger, the one that was clawing, and clumps flew up into Short's face. Short's body jerked, and he hollered loud, long, and strong.

Tall came to, raised himself up, checked out what was happening, and passed out again.

"Where the money?" George said, over Short's screams.

Between screams and when he could catch a bit of air, Short called me some really nasty names. I got even and gave him a good one for Seltzer. I applied pressure to his broken leg with my foot and heard more bones snap. His scream was horrendous, but he deserved it.

George got jealous, pushed me out of the way, and took over the torture. And, I have to admit, George was more focused about it.

He demanded that Short tell him where the money was while he inflicted pain, which made me happy, I can tell you, because he ignored Short's accusations leveled at me. In true gangster fashion George prepared to beat the information out of Short.

And I stood by, watching justice at work. See, Short had made a big mistake when he knocked George out night before last, and George wasn't forgetting it. And I wasn't forgetting that George had knocked *me* out last night.

Everybody was getting theirs. Payback is a bitch, ain't it?

In no time at all, Short sang like a canary bird. He mentioned a boat, a slip number, and where the money was stashed. Well, my job was done. Time to split.

I walked over to Stepchild. She looked like somebody's foster child now, her chassis in horrible condition, all bent and warped. I prepared to give her last rites, and without much hope, I climbed into the car on the passenger side and patted and stroked her dashboard. On an impulse, I inserted the key in the ignition. Hot damn, her old engine roared to life, and Foster Child hummed and purred like a pussy.

And then I was dragged out of the car, my wrists tied with someone's belt, and thrown into another limping car and we headed to the docks. George wasn't through with me yet.

Chapter 44

In the marina only a few boats bumped hulls against the dock, their owners absent. The rest of the boats had gone to join the Tall Ships, celebrants in the bicentennial armada that filled the harbor—Operation Sail a roaring success. Fireworks burst in the air, and sizzled and spurted, lighting up the Manhattan skyline and bringing sight and sound to this deserted Bronx inlet and this thirty-two-foot cabin cruiser in which I was currently imprisoned.

Short lay moaning on a bunk against the wall. George had discovered the booze early on and him and his men worked on three bottles of gin, scotch, and vodka sitting on top of the kitchenette's counter. Me and Tall were handcuffed to each other—and believe me, neither of us was happy about that.

Tall's breath smelled like rank garbage, and we sat facing each other across a dinette table, two sets of cuffs locking us together. George's brain had short-circuited, a trust issue, I think, and he wasn't letting me go. Where was Bundt when I needed him?

George and two of his men stayed belowdecks to guard us—it was crowded—and four more wandered above us, oohing and ahing at the fireworks and playing with the boat's engine. Every so often the boat's motor came to life, sputtered, then died out, and the Clots had great fun laughing and carrying on.

You can bet I didn't see the humor. On this Fourth of July, with everyone celebrating freedom, I had just lost mine, and suspected my life was pretty much in jeopardy as well.

So far George had trashed the cabin in an unorganized search and come up with only twenty keys of heroin and no money. I'd bet there was more, but I was prevented from joining in the search by the manacles on my wrist. Besides, George didn't deserve my cooperation after the way he treated me.

Tall started negotiating. "Look, if my partner and I don't report in soon, somebody's going to start looking for us. Kidnapping federal agents? Life without the possibility of parole. They'll bury you *under* the jail."

"Yeah?" said George. "And what if them agents get killed and can't nobody find their bodies? How much we get for that?"

Tall squirmed in his seat. "You got the heroin. What else do you want?"

"Where the money? Anyway, this one say the H is no good. What you got to say about that?"

"*This* one"—Tall indicated me and jerked my wrist—"is lying. There's nothing wrong with the dope. And I told you, I don't keep money on board. For what? The money's deposited in a bank."

I kept my mouth shut, but I doubted he was telling the truth. In the bank, ha! George looked at me the way you'd study a bug and said, "One way to find out."

He tore open a bag of heroin and sniffed. Then he rubbed it between his fingers. Then he whispered to his Clots and the two disappeared. George stood, hunched over, in the alcove of the small kitchenette and waited.

A few minutes passed, and then Tall asked, "What are we waiting for?"

"Syringe." And then George smiled.

Tall and I got it at the same time. No peep out of Short, he was wrapped up in pain.

"You're not going to inject us with that shit, are you?" Tall said.

I jumped in with my two cents, and winked at George. "If if ain't poison, what's the big deal? A little nod, and it's over with."

"Are you out of your mind? These idiots might kill us with an overdose and still not know if the skag was good or not."

I leaned toward George. "You know, George, he's got a point. Better give those two just a little pop."

George rested his pudgy hands on his belly and said, "Gone give you *all* a pop. How you like that? Know soon enough who's lying."

I blanched. He was serious. "George. You ain't thinking right. Harry ain't going to like it if his duke gets offed. Better check with him before you do anything rash."

The smile on George's face twisted and turned mean. "You ain't a duke yet."

I'll be damned, I thought, *George is jealous—of me*. Tall got hysterical and tried to climb out of his seat, but to do it he had to drag me with him and it wasn't happening. George backhanded him, and he crashed back onto the bench.

Down the stairs came a skinny Clot, paraphernalia in hand. He set about—all businesslike—preparing the stuff, cooked it over a burner on the cabin's stove, and then he wrapped a belt around Short's arm, and Short got the first injection. Probably a relief to Short, who, earlier, had been groveling in pain on the bunk.

Next they shot up Tall and he didn't go down without a struggle. Whadda ya know? He probably believed the stuff was poison too. It took a minute before Tall's eyes glazed over and he relaxed into his seat.

Mind over matter. I licked my lips and started my own negotiating. "Look, George, it'd look bad for a fellow countryman to be found dead with a dress on. Not good for our image." Owning up to the fact I was part Monkey Chaser was not as difficult as I thought. Acceptance, when you know the truth, didn't have to be a pill to swallow. I shook my head, to focus on the now. "How about you let me take this dress off?"

A puzzled look started in George's forehead and moved to his eyes. He nodded, hauled me up, and roughly pulled the dress over my head and down my arms. Then he suddenly realized he'd have to uncuff me to finish the job. He searched Tall's pockets for the keys, dangled them in the air at me, and then threw them across the room. Okay, to be honest I didn't think he'd go for it, but hey, I had to try. George signaled to the skinny Clot; he belted me up and I steeled myself for the needle.

Mind over matter. Nothing and nobody could touch me. I felt it when it hit—hands pulled me down into a long, dark tunnel. Across the table Tall started heaving and dry-retching. George jumped into action, undid one of the cuffs, and hauled Tall to the tiny bathroom, me stumbling after, and stuffed Tall's head in the toilet. Just in time, the vomit exploded out of Tall, and George jumped over me to miss it. I slumped on the floor with my back against the door, waves of peace and contentment rippling through my body. No wonder junkies liked this, I thought. I tried to focus and keep my mind sharp, but I lost it and drifted down a river.

I *was* moving down a river. When I opened my eyes, I felt the movement of the boat, the hum of the engine. No Clots in the cabin—their shouts and laughter rang out up on the deck. Tall's head rested against the commode, his body stuffed into the small space, one long leg bent under the sink and the other one stretched out the door and laid across my crotch. I moved his skinny leg and thumped his shoulder to bring him around. No luck.

I struggled to my feet, still dizzy and in a twilight zone, and grabbed him and dragged him with me over to a porthole and looked out. The boat was speeding across the water. No surrounding boats were going this fast. What the fuck—the Clots were joyriding? Surely this boat would be stopped.

Band music played nearby. I moved to the opposite porthole. Jesus. We were in Lower Manhattan. The carrier USS *Forrestal* was all lit up—we were about a mile from the dock. Limbs heavy, I fought to remain alert and searched the cabin for the keys to the handcuffs. Then I tried both Short's and Tall's pocket again. Nothing. I looked up. George must have taken them.

The drug kept trying to take over my body. I didn't let it. I weighed more than the other two—maybe that was the reason. I stumbled about the cabin, searching for life jackets. I found six of them in a hatch above the galley. I unrolled two, and what did I find in the pockets of one of the vests? Money, that's what. Lots and lots of it. Way more than a hundred thousand, I'd bet my watch. I wrapped the vest around me and buckled it tight. Then I put another vest on top of that one—as best I was able, since only one arm could go through. I secured it, hoping to hell it wouldn't come off. Then I put a life jacket on Tall.

The Clots caroused above me. They sang, "Oh, say, can you see?" while the band played.

I was inflating Tall's vest when out of the corner of my eye I noticed Winnie's purse lying on the floor under the dinette table. Hoping against hope, I reached for it and opened it. The guns were there. No one had bothered to look inside. Thank you, God. I just became a believer. I took the loaded one, Harry's 35 mm, and stuffed it in the top of the vest.

Then I hauled Tall to his knees and slapped his cheeks a few times. He needed to be on his feet if we were going to do this.

I kept my voice low. "Listen, Mr. DEA Dope Dealer, if you want to get out of this alive, you'd better follow instructions. You have to make it up those stairs, hear me?" I shook him hard. "You have to."

His eyes rolled around in his head, but he seemed to know what I was saying. I pulled him to his feet. He leaned against me. This wasn't going to work. "Damn it, stand up," I hissed. I shook him again. "We're going up those stairs and when we get to the top, we have to jump overboard, hear me?"

He nodded, he understood. But then he looked over at his partner; I snapped his head back around again. "If we get out alive, maybe we can help him. But for now we got to leave him."

I moved to the bottom of the steps and he followed on his own steam, then began to wilt to the floor. I grabbed him by the collar and held him up. I pulled him up the stairs, gun poised in front of me, ready to shoot. "Let's go," I shouted and fired four rounds as I broke through the opening at the top of the stairs.

The Clots were slow to react. George reached clumsily for his gun, and two Clots hit the deck. The others bumped into each other, confused. I fired another round, dropped the gun, grabbed Tall by the shoulders, and heaved him over the edge of the boat. He sailed through the air and I sailed after, both of us plunging into the cold waters of the Hudson.

Chapter 45

The Hudson River animated both of us. The water shocked us and got our attention. We floundered in the backwash from the craft vessel, gulping for air and spitting out river water. Bound together, we had no choice but to cooperate with each other. After some tentative tries we got our act together and began stroking through the water in rhythm. A yacht two hundred feet away with music coming from it had couples dancing on its deck, watching the fireworks, heads tilted toward the night sky. Our shouts went unheard over the music, and the yacht was moving away from us. To our left a cabin cruiser, the *Tilloo III*, larger than the one we had left, was being piloted by a bearded man sitting high up on its bridge and about the same distance away, but this vessel was moving toward us. Without words Tall and I made the decision at the same time and we swam toward it.

All the boats traveled in the same direction down the river—all of them, except the boat we had just leaped from. It made a wide circle in the water and was now coming back for us. I could see its name across the left bow, the *Money Changer*.

Tall and I put on as much steam as we could muster, stroking faster and faster, but the waves from the oncoming vessel lapped over us, submerging us time and again. We were directly in its path and had to get to the other side—put it between us and the Clots.

Tall was near drowned and so was I, but I kept fighting to get to the lee side of *Tilloo III*.

Gunshots popped in the air behind us. "C'mon, asshole, stroke," I yelled to Tall. *Tilloo III* slowed; its owner blasted its horn and yelled through a megaphone to the Clots to turn their boat around. The Clots ignored him. Other boats noticed the offending boat and joined in the act. They too called, honked, and chastised.

What the Clots didn't want was to call attention to themselves. They veered the boat around once more and headed back down the Hudson. Tall and I made it to the other side of the *Tilloo* and waved our arms and shouted, lungs bursting with the effort. *Tilloo*'s owner spied us in the water, idled his engine, and threw out two life preservers. A woman appeared at the boat's railing and helped to haul us in.

We flopped on the deck of the *Tilloo* like two spent sharks. The woman shrieked when she noticed the handcuffs, and the man immediately grabbed a gaff and held it overhead—to protect himself, I guess, from two handcuffed men.

Tall and I pointed accusing fingers at each other and the couple's gazes jerked back and forth between the two of us as if they were watching a Ping-Pong match.

Finally, Tall dug inside his jacket and pulled out his badge. The couple was impressed, I could tell, and cast dark looks at me as if I were a serial killer or something. Graybeard shifted his body and pointed the gaff at my chest.

"Hold it," I said. "If you don't believe me, call the Twenty-eighth Precinct, ask to speak to Detective Bundt. He'll straighten this out. This man is a criminal."

Tall spoke up, authority in his voice. "Get me something to break these handcuffs. I'm a federal agent with the Drug Enforcement Agency and this man is my prisoner. I'll need to use your radio." Graybeard hesitated for an instant, but Wifey disappeared below and returned within minutes with a gun, leveled at me. Guess a suit and a badge beats out a nigger in his underwear any day. Should I have been surprised?

Her hands shook and I thought, *Don't let her hiccup*. Her husband found a hammer and placed the boat's anchor between us and hammered on the cuffs with all his might. It took a while, but they finally split.

Tall got up, eased the gun out of Wifey's hand, and said, "I'm taking over. Stand back, all of you."

Oh, shit no . . . out of the frying pan into the . . . I lunged at Tall's knees, knocked him over, and he hit his head. I didn't wait. I leaped, once again, into the breach and over the side, and this time, made it to shore.

I scaled rocks, people in the crowd lifted me to safety, and I disappeared quickly among the thousands of people that lined the pier.

Chapter 46

I loved New York. Dressed as I was in a life vest, with only my undershirt on and wet pants, and half of a handcuff attached to my left hand, nobody looked at me twice as I walked the streets in search of a phone booth. When I found one that wasn't broken, I stopped a passing teenager and exchanged a fifty I had pulled out of the vest for some change.

I called Bundt, and of course, he wasn't there—not on July 4, a holiday. I left a life-and-death message along with the names of the two boats with a Sergeant Willis, gave him my first name only and told him Bundt could reach me at home in about an hour. I hung up before Willis could ask questions. Then since no son-of-a-bitching taxi driver would pick me up, I took the A-train home.

Thirty minutes later I was walking down my block, doing the last mile, as head down, I avoided the smiles, pats on the back, and applause of the neighbors. My cheeks were burning. They even waved their red, white, and blue flags at me. If you want to know the truth I was mortified. I entered my brownstone and shut them out.

A few hours of sleep revived me somewhat and I called Steadwell, told him to pick me up at 4:00 A.M., and together we made Stepchild disappear from the Bronx alley before anybody investigated.

Steadwell harangued that I had to make things right with Harry if I wanted to stay alive and remain in Harlem. I told him I didn't have to do anything but stay black and die. I told him I'd give Harry back his money and call it quits.

Like a send-off at a funeral, Steadwell wished me luck and dropped me at the hospital where Seltzer was staying, said he was going back home to get some sleep. I thanked him and went up see Seltzer. Selz was awake, couldn't talk much, still had tubes coming out of every which way. I let him know what had happened and saw a glimmer of a smile through the bandages. I stayed a little longer, and when Seltzer's wife showed up, I said good-bye and left.

At a coffee shop a block from the hospital I stopped and bought a couple of newspapers. Bicentennial news filled most of the front sections, the drug bust was relegated to the back pages. The papers said seven black men were arrested as principal suspects in a drug ring, and were likewise responsible for the homicide slaying of one Ezekiel Johnson. Ain't that a blip? No mention of the DEA boys.

With liberty and justice for all—no alphabet agency mentioned, but the Coast Guard, the Maritime Police and the NYPD and Lieutenant Bundt were labeled heroes. I smiled. I was okay with that. Guess I wouldn't be hearing from Bundt.

I put in a call to Catherine, didn't give a lot of details, but I let her know I was all right and headed back home.

As I rounded the corner of my block I bumped into the pastor and some of his flock, standing in front of the entrance to his church. Somebody's funeral? The pastor shook his head and said, "Not yet." It didn't take long to figure out that the funeral might be mine.

Neighbors lined the block on either side, on sidewalks and stoops. I strode past them, my footsteps keeping time to the thumping of my heart. I kept walking. The way I figured it, if a man is any kind of a man, sometime in his life he has to stand for something. The skeletons that nested in my head had been removed and for the first time in a long while I was clear about a lot of things.

Finding out that Zeke was my real father—I knew that I wasn't anything like him, and never would be—lifted a huge weight from my shoulders. What I came from didn't have a damn thing to do with who I was.

Familiar faces called to me. My neighbors began to reach for me, pat me on the back, and shake my hand. My people, my Harlem. Hell, these people were closer to anything I ever knew of family.

Up ahead Harry and his army sat waiting, five cars of them, four black Lincolns and one shiny gold Cadillac. My tenants were out in front, crowded together in front of both brownstones, Wilbur leading them in a cheer. A sting in my nostril reminded me I had friends.

When I was almost on them, the Clots poured out of their cars, black spiders loosed from their cocoons—and Harry the Monkey Chaser led the pack.

He shouted, "Amos, didn't think you were going to get away with it, did you?"

Youngblood, my former tenant, crawled out of one of Harry's cars like the cockroach he was and stood behind Harry, triumph on his face.

"I got back your money, Harry. Take it and go."

"It ain't about the money."

I smiled. "I know, Harry, I know, it's about the glory." I told Wilbur my apartment door was open, and to go inside and bring the life jacket laying on the coffee table. "The money's in it," I said to Harry. Wilbur handed off Josie to Winnie and hurriedly did as I asked.

Harry and his crew walked toward me and I told my tenants to head indoors. Winnie bundled the baby up and went into the house. The other tenants stayed where they were. I didn't move, I waited for Harry, ready to take anything he wanted to hand out. When Harry and I at last stood toe to toe I said, "When you get the money, that's it, Harry. I don't want any part of you or your operation."

"You queered the deal on purpose, didn't you? Here I was, ready to bring you into the fold like a brother, and you fucked up—big time. Nobody crosses Harry."

"What can I say? You're right, Harry. Can't go the drug route. It ain't in me—ain't that kind of person. I can't destroy the place where I live. Can't do that to my people."

Harry's eyes turned mean. "You can't, huh? Ain't that a piss-ass shame. I got casualties—casualties, seven good men—and it gone cost you. *All* your marbles, you hear me?"

I shrugged. "Your boys were stupid, Harry—greedy too. Not my fault."

Harry sucker punched me in the stomach and I dropped to the pavement on one knee. Then he signaled to his men. They hauled gas cans out of their cars. I jumped to my feet and threw a right, smack into Harry's wide-open face. The punch surprised him and, splat, Harry's face opened like a watermelon splitting. It was Harry's turn to hit the ground, and he screamed bloody murder.

Then I lost my mind, I jumped on top of Harry and started pounding. The Clots pulled me off him and did the same number on me. Blows rained down on my face, shoulders, stomach. I saw stars—a whole galaxy. They had me down and began kicking.

Wilbur tried to pull the Clots off and got knocked down for his trouble. At the same time, a taxi pulled up, horn honking. A noise began in the street and voices rose in protest. People screamed at Harry and his Clots. A wave of people pushed the Clots back, and off of me.

Then I heard glass break and I smelled smoke. I struggled to my feet. Flames licked out of my office window. Fear gripped me—*Josephine and Winnie* were in the brownstone. I pushed past bodies and charged up the front steps.

In front of the door was a Clot throwing gasoline on the building. I kicked the gasoline can out of his hand and pushed him over the railing. I dashed through the entrance to my brownstone. Smoke was rolling out of the office and up the stairwell. My eyes burned and I started hacking from the smoke. I took off my undershirt, held it against my nose and mouth, and ascended the stairwell.

I heard Winnie call out on the landing above and I shouted, "Hang on, Winnie, I'm coming. Easy does it. Take it easy." Winnie inched step by step down the stairs, carrying her small charge like precious cargo. Every black person knew that with sickle-cell anemia, one bruise to Josie's body could put her back in the hospital, so Winnie was coming down the stairs slowly and carefully. I ran up the stairs to meet them.

And then hallelujah, miracles of miracles, a whoosh of water fell, the sprinklers finally kicked in, and steam and smoke filled the stairwell. Guess it was worth the money after all, but I could hardly see in front of me. I took Josie from Winnie. "Hang on to the banister going down, Winnie, you'll be okay."

I shielded the baby's face and carried her the rest of the way. When we reached the street, it was in total chaos. The cab was blocked and couldn't move. A throng of people pushed and pulled, some in mortal battle with the Clots. Bottles, glass, and rocks were thrown. Catherine and her mother stood off to the side, at the edge of the crowd. Catherine saw me and started to press forward through the melee, but she was pushed back. I couldn't get to her either.

Wilbur, bleeding, his shirt ripped, tore himself away from the action, rescued Josie, and carried her to safety, a distance away from the crowd.

Miss Ellie and others behind her—even Gloria—chanted on the sidewalk, "No more drugs, no more drugs." Harry, with the yellow life jacket slung over his shoulder, looked like a giant bumblebee, raving hysterically.

This had to end. I took off after him. He saw me coming and raced to his gold Cadillac and reached inside and came out with a grenade in his hand.

"Hold it, Amos." Harry wheezed, and sweat crawled down his face. "Tell all these people to stop, or me gone use this, and you know I will."

I looked Harry in the eye and stepped forward. Someone screamed behind me.

Grenade held high, Harry reached into his waistband and pulled out a piece and said, "I'll kill you first and blow everybody sky-high."

"That right, Harry? Blast everybody? Women, children—your sister and niece too?" People quieted behind me. They could see what was happening.

Harry held the grenade still higher and searched the crowd for sight of Mrs. Walters and Catherine, his breathing heavy. "Over there, Harry. Next to the cab." Harry's eyes darted left and saw the two making their way through the crowd.

Sirens sounded in the distance. Harry had to make a decision.

The cops would be here soon. I pressed my advantage. "If it's about winning, Harry, you won, you got your money back, you put a hurting on my buildings. Ain't that enough?"

From where I stood I could see the muscles twitching in Harry's face, his eyes filled with rage. Harry wheezed and pointed the gun straight at my chest. "No," he said, and fired.

Chapter 47

Shocked, I looked to where Harry lay on the ground. Catherine sobbed beside me. For sure, I thought I was good as dead. Wilbur had saved my life and fired a rock at Harry's head, knocking Harry for a loop, his shot going wild.

Catherine's mother jabbered double time over Harry's prostrate body, rolling out that West Indian patois so fast I couldn't understand her. Then she turned and hugged me, pressed a red bag into my hand, and dropped to the ground to minister to Harry.

In disbelief, the crowd edged closer to the fallen King of Harlem. I moved them back and knelt beside a wheezing Harry, his face covered with blood, and said, "I'm putting you in your car, Harry. But this is the deal—this street is out of bounds to you and yours, Harry, drug-free, understand?"

Harry choked on his rage. "You punk . . . you don't give Harry orders. This street, she be junkie heaven, if me want it. Me boys will—"

"Your boys ain't around, Harry." I helped him to his feet, and the red bag fell to the ground beside him. He jumped back and screamed as if I stabbed him, and his scream set off my key chain. "Here I am, here I am," it proclaimed.

He screamed again, louder this time. I don't know what the hell Harry thought was happening. I guess he thought some voodoo god was speaking in another voice. Harry backed up, pressed against his car, and yelled to beat the band.

I pinned him against the car while the key chain was still talking, and said, "No drugs, understand?"

"No drugs," Harry whispered, the sound barely escaping his lips. The key chain went silent and I stood Harry up. Once upright, he shook me off, mustered what dignity he could, gestured to his Clots, and they piled into their respective cars. "Until next time, Amos."

I called after him, "Won't be no next time, Harry."

He indicated the red bag of gris-gris on the ground and smiled. "Eh-eh . . . just like your father?"

I narrowed my eyes. So Harry knew, too. "No, Harry, not like my father. Make no mistake, I ain't that kind of fool." And Harry and his hoods drove away.

I surveyed the damage. Could have been worse. People returned to their homes. Some stayed to help with the cleanup. I gathered my tenants around and announced, "Third floors, basements in both places are okay. Parlor floors need work, but I can deal with that. Mostly smoke damage and broken windows. You're welcome to move to any available apartment that's livable if yours is messed up. Couple of neighbors said their homes would be open to you until I can get the brownstones back in order."

And then I thanked them for their support and I meant it. This group was family—I cared about each one of them and they seemed to know it. My only regret was Patty, and that troubled me. I hoped she was still alive.

Then, out of the blue, Gloria threw her arms around me, with Catherine standing right there too, and said, "Oh, Amos, darling, I was so frightened for you."

Now, Gloria ain't never in her life called me darling; I looked at her as if she had lost her mind. But the woman liked to perform, should have been an actress, and I'm sure she knew something was up with Catherine. Catherine moved back to let Gloria have full rein and crossed her arms—a sure sign of trouble. Mrs. Walters looked back and forth at the two women.

I tried to unpeel Gloria, but she stuck to me like glue. I made the introductions with Gloria hanging off my neck—what else could I do? And it was all over for me then. Catherine told me she'd leave me to my *wife*—she put an extra zing in the word *wife*—told me to have a good life, she never wanted to speak to me again, and to top if off, called me Harlem trash. Can you believe it? The niece of a notorious drug dealer called *me* Harlem trash.

Well, I told her straight out I had another woman anyway, that I planned to see her later tonight. Gloria was shocked, that got her off me, but Catherine was more shocked, and she and her mom left right after in the cab. Wilbur, standing on the sidelines with Josie still in his arms, pursed his lips together and just looked at me, disgust in his eyes.

I'd call it a tension breaker. Life can't be all bad if two women are upset with you. The neighbors bade their farewells and slipped away into their homes, and the street soon folded in on itself. Business as usual on 128th Street.

Inside my burned office, I glanced at the charred photo gallery. The unknown woman's picture was the only photo that had survived. Only the glass was broken. Probably an aunt, grandmother, or cousin of Montcrieff's, not related to me at all. Huh, not related to me at all. I swept all of the pictures into the wastebasket and with the gesture bade the woman a fond farewell. She'd served her purpose and it was time to say good-bye.

I stood for several minutes in that room with my hands in my pockets, not doing anything, really—thinking. The floor was soppy wet, the smoke strong, and I felt bone tired, deep down to my soul. But I had things to do yet. I roused myself, went to the cellar, and found wood, nails, and a hammer to board up the broken windows in both brownstones. ". . . and miles to go . . ."

Ten minutes later on the subway platform, I waited for the number 2 train to Brooklyn. The last stop.

Chapter 48

Reba knew the jig was up soon as I came through her front door. Her face ashen, she didn't look well at all. What was it about Reba? The first thing she asked, did I want something to eat? Quietly I said, "Like what you fed Zeke? My father?"

Reba swayed on her feet. I caught her and halfway carried her into the kitchen and deposited her into a kitchen chair. Then I got water from her refrigerator and gave it to her. She cried like a baby. Silent, I stared at a spot somewhere above her head, and waited for the waterfall to cease.

"Zeke was an evil, vile man," she said, and a fresh wave of sobs overtook her. "I never meant to hurt you, I swear I didn't."

"Start at the beginning, Reba."

"Zeke and I had just begun to . . . court. That's what we called it in those days. Zeke introduced me to Montcrieff, his best friend, and I introduced Zeke to mine, my sister . . . That's when the trouble started."

I pulled no punches. "Zeke and my mother were lovers."

Reba straightened her spine and pulled herself up.

"Yes, later. The four of us double-dated, went everywhere together. One day, I caught my sister and Zeke together. It was bad. I saw red, blamed my sister. We never spoke after that. Never. Then she suddenly up and married Montcrieff. And Zeke came back to me."

"After what he did to you, you wanted him?" I said.

Reba broke down, her tears marking a path down her chin and into the folds of her neck. "He was my sickness, you see?" She wanted absolution. She looked to me as if I were a father confessor. I could only stare at her, and wonder.

"Caught them again—after Elizabeth was married." Reba pressed her hand against her chest, the pain so deep inside her it seemed to make her heart ache and stop her speech. "Elizabeth in Zeke's old house, crying, Zeke slobbering all over her. I—I was angry, jealous. It wasn't fair. Three months before, she had given birth to you. Started hitting her, she didn't even defend herself. Fell, against the basement door. It gave way and she tumbled down the steps. . . . I was shocked . . . so still, she just lay there. Zeke said I'd killed her—told me to get out of there before Montcrieff found her. I left her lying there, went back home, and never saw my sister again."

"Zeke told you what he did with the body?"

"No, never. I didn't want to know. He made up a lie for Montcrieff —to protect me, I thought. Told him Elizabeth had run off with another man. They were best friends. Montcrieff believed him. It broke Montcrieff's heart. I couldn't say no when he asked me to raise you."

"You never raised me, Reba, you let me grow up in the same house as you. It ain't the same thing."

A fresh gush of tears poured from Reba's eyes. "Every time I looked into your face I saw Elizabeth looking back at me. I couldn't take it. I missed my sister. I wanted to sell the house and move away."

She dabbed at her nose with a lace handkerchief taken from her pocket. I grabbed her arm, paper-thin between my fingers, and said, "But you couldn't do that, could you, until your sister was declared dead? That's the only reason you reported her missing."

Reba spat back at me, "No. I reported her missing when I found out you was Zeke's kid."

"Montcrieff told you, didn't he? When I was seven. That's when he changed his will."

Reba's eyes widened. "Montcrieff knew Elizabeth had been raped, but it was years before he suspected Zeke. Even then, he forgave him, but he always blamed him for Elizabeth's disappearance. He never knew Elizabeth was dead. But he did his duty by you. Every month without fail he gave me money for your keep, anything you needed. I think he loved you."

"Reba, he never had anything to do with me. How in hell did you figure he loved me?"

"That part don't matter. He cared about you. Better that than someone that never owned up to being your father, that never loved nobody 'cause they too busy loving themself up."

"Talking about Zeke?" I said.

Reba nodded. "He killed her, you know. When you told me she had been strangled, that's when I knew. The crushed bones in her neck . . . cemented my sister up in that wall . . . When you saw us the other day in my kitchen? Zeke admitted it—and he laughed about it. Laughed . . . to my face."

"That's why you killed him."

"Lies. Made me believe I killed my own sweet sister, held it over my head all these years. He was the one wouldn't leave Elizabeth alone. Deep down I knew that, always knew that. Her trying to do the right thing, and he wouldn't let her. I know that now. He killed her because she threatened to tell Montcrieff everything, and he was depending on Montcrieff to bail him out on his house."

"The bottle of rum?"

"Yes. It didn't take no effort. Mixed a potion, poured it in the rum, and gave it to Zeke. For over thirty years I growed that man's herbs, gave him money every time he needed it, cooked his meals. He leaned on me for years, and lied to me just as long."

I sighed. She looked at me. "He would have destroyed you too, you know, and I couldn't let him do that."

Like a balloon deflating, Reba shrank into herself and we sat, quiet as growing grass, deep in our own thoughts, as day broke into a thousand pieces and crumbled away.

I mused, Reba threw her life away—for nothing. Well, I was determined not to make that mistake. Outside, the twilight deepened and Reba made no move to turn the light on. Finally I brushed o my pants and got up to go.

Reba said, "I'm gonna call the police, turn myself in."

I looked down at her. "Why, Reba? What good would it

"Police will be looking for me."

"For Zeke's death? No, I don't think so. They're looking at drug dealers. Won't find them, but they'll be looking."

"Amos? Stay to dinner?" she asked.

I looked at her frail body and a surge of the first real feeling I ever felt for Reba surfaced. Too bad it was pity. I declined the invitation, and left that house and Reba. On the porch, Reba's rhododendrons had lost their spirit—like the woman inside, drooped over and bent. They were wilting from the July heat. She must have forgotten. I picked up a watering can, filled it with water, and the flowers greedily sucked it up. As I left that house for the last time they lifted their leaves in farewell.

Chapter 49

I was exhausted beyond belief, my eyes scratchy, and I was almost dizzy from lack of sleep. But I had to do this. It didn't take long to locate Hocks at her stomping grounds in front of the Mount Zion Temple of God, and with some prodding, she led me to a place in Harlem that resembled a WWI bomb site, which even she scurried away from. Her Hockness wouldn't be caught dead in a place like this. I wondered if my search would be futile.

The smell of garbage and decay around the building's perimeter offended, the sight depressed. The reality mirrored my remembered nightmares when I was surrounded by stench and filth. In front of me was the embodiment of that dream, a former hotel that housed the lowest of the low, the addict. Its waste and rubble reeked. From where I stood, it appeared to be unoccupied. Nothing stirred.

I fidgeted on the street, making up my mind. Patty couldn't be here. I walked away, but got no farther than half a block before I changed my mind again and turned back. I couldn't face myself in the mirror if I didn't at least make a stab at finding the girl.

The chances of succeeding were about a million to one. Even for a gambler like me, the odds stank. Patty might be anywhere, even downtown, in alphabet city. Ironic, wasn't it, the fabled borough of Manhattan, book-ended uptown and down by two drug hamlets?

But as Ham Hocks pointed out to me, this building wasn't far from the neighborhood, so maybe . . .

My skin itched in distaste. I climbed over I don't know what-all piled high around the outside of the building. It occurred to me I might be stepping on someone's remains hidden under the rubbish. In a place like this, it was possible.

I stepped through a hole whose opening was larger than the door beside it. The gloom inside contrasted sharply with the brightness of outdoors. I went deep into the interior and couldn't see my hands in front of me. My fingers touched the walls, which offered braille directions to where I headed. Skittering noises around me let me know the rodents had been disturbed.

I made my way through ink, down a hallway, stumbled over something lying in my path, caught my balance, and jumped back in horror. A body of a woman lay stretched across the concrete floor. Cautiously, I knelt beside the body and turned it over. Shit, the woman was breathing. I shook her. She smiled a lazy smile. I let her drop. Stoned out of her mind. I wiped my hand on my pants.

Above me I heard noises. My eyes had gotten used to the dark and I found the staircase, next to an elevator shaft, and climbed to the second floor. I inched along the corridor, ears alert, listening for sounds, and turned right. At the far end of the hallway, a door stood open. I moved forward and entered a suite of rooms.

The most god-awful sight greeted me. Zombie junkies sat on the floor, leaning against faded rose-patterned walls, nodding, or sleeping on rotted mattresses. Broken needles littered the room. Hard to believe, but two people in the corner were fucking, unconcerned about an audience, their rhythm lazy and loose.

I described Patty and asked if anyone had seen her. All I got was an "it's all good" from an emaciated "Rufus" slouched near the door. I pulled a bill from my pocket. Wrong thing to do. Two of the more alive zombies stirred, eyes snapping to attention, their bodies agitated. They jabbered separate lies at the same time. In stereophonic sound, talking shit. Junkies will tell you anything. It was no use. I threw a five-dollar bill into the center of the room and turned to go. Three of them lunged for the bill, like dogs after a bone. I left and hustled back down the hall to the stairs.

Coming down, I heard movement behind me. I turned just in

time. Rufus had followed me. He reached for me. I knocked away his arm, grabbed his shirt, and threw him headfirst down the stairs. He rolled and bumped past me, his knife clattering to the floor. What the fuck was I doing here? I picked up the mean-looking stiletto, closed it, and slid it into my pocket. I ran down the rest of the stairs, before the zombie horde above got the same idea, stepped over his body, and strode out of the building.

Not until I was several blocks away did I begin to shake the experience. Harlem at its worst. I hoped to God that Patty wasn't in a place like that.

Chapter 50

I surfaced at Lenox Boulevard, stood and looked up and down the street. Street sounds, a vibrant symphony, accosted my ears. I watched people drift past me, smiles on their faces, their energies raising my own. In spite of everything, in spite of the casualties like Patty, this was a people that survived. Could I do any less?

Okay, so my buildings were trashed. They could be fixed. Josie was without a mother. Wilbur was on the case. My relationship with Catherine was in the toilet. That could be mended. I stank. A bath could fix that. Harry was out of my hair. Ahh . . .

My mood altered. I chuckled, and that felt good. And then James Brown started singing in my head—*I feel good.* Yep, in spite of everything, I did feel good. On an impulse, I kicked my leg, spun around, and squealed, and was rewarded with more than a few stares.

Never mind. I tipped through Harlem, light as a biscuit. The night air was an Easter Bunny, all soft and warm and close around me. Nights like these were made for fools like me. Life was kind, and people were good. I followed my feet and let them lead me.

I felt good.

Hey, Brother-Man, how you doing, son? Evening, sweet Mama. Yo, cool, how it is? Greetings rippled from a sea of faces, in this, my Harlem Village.

And you know, walking wasn't such a bad thing. Catherine's apartment was west and that's where I was headed. When she opened the door in her robe and I asked to see her mama, she was speechless. I took advantage of that and laid a big one on her, her lips soft and full under mine. Trash indeed. Never mind what her schooling had taught her up to this point, this woman was about to receive a full-blown education from this Harlem brother, a-what-you-say, don't-take-no-stuff, Nigger Landlord.

A READING GROUP GUIDE

A LANDLORD'S TALE

GAMMY L. SINGER

ABOUT THIS GUIDE

The suggested questions are intended to enhance your group's reading of Gammy L. Singer's A LANDLORD'S TALE.

DISCUSSION QUESTIONS

1. When does *A Landlord's Tale* take place? What details in the novel help you to understand that?

2. Is Amos Brown someone you'd like to know? Why or why not?

3. Amos makes a few mistakes. Which one is the most egregious and why do you think so?

4. What character, other than Amos, is a favorite? Explain why.

5. Amos has prejudices. Discuss them in terms of the time period of the novel and how his prejudices might be viewed today.

6. Why might Harlem be considered another character in the novel?

7. Before you read *A Landlord's Tale*, did you have opinions about Harlem? Have these opinions changed? Describe the Harlem of that era as the author envisioned it.

8. What was Amos's journey in this story? How was he different at the end of the story as opposed to the beginning?

9. What character did you have the most sympathy for?

10. Were you disappointed that Harry the Monkey Chaser's drug business was allowed to continue? Do you think it was a realistic ending? What ending would you have constructed?